John Stuart Ogilvie

The American Temperance Speaker

John Stuart Ogilvie

The American Temperance Speaker

ISBN/EAN: 9783337371661

Printed in Europe, USA, Canada, Australia, Japan

Cover: Foto ©Andreas Hilbeck / pixelio.de

More available books at **www.hansebooks.com**

THE AMERICAN
TEMPERANCE SPEAKER,
No. 1.

A CHOICE COLLECTION OF

DIALOGUES, PROSE AND POETRY,

ESPECIALLY ADAPTED FOR USE IN ALL

Adult and Juvenile Temperance Organizations,

SABBATH AND DAY SCHOOLS,

AND FOR

PUBLIC AND PRIVATE READINGS, RECITATIONS AND ADDRESSES.

Compiled by J. S. OGILVIE.

NEW YORK:

𝕬merican 𝕿emperance 𝕻ublishing 𝕳ouse,

29 ROSE STREET.

1879.

PREFACE.

MANY persons will, doubtless, ask why it is that another book of Recitations and Speeches is sent forth to the public to receive from it their verdict of approval or disapproval. Our reply is, that we feel that this collection fills a place, and supplies a demand, which has not been filled before to any extent; and hope that, as this is sent forth to aid in advancing the great Temperance Reform, all friends of the cause everywhere will feel it a privilege to aid in its wide circulation, and place it in the possession of all Temperance Organizations, both Adult and Juvenile, as well as in Sabbath and Day Schools. Should this collection meet with public favor, another one will follow in due time.

Any friend of the cause, desiring to contribute original or selected articles to such a collection, may forward them to the Publisher.

CONTENTS.

RULES TO BE OBSERVED IN RECITING.

RULE 1.—Stand erect; hold up your head manfully; keep a full supply of breath; and speak according to the nature of the subject you recite.

RULE 2.—To recite well, you must pronounce every word distinctly and correctly. To do this, open your mouth, and move your tongue and lips freely.

RULE 3.—Be careful to give the vowels their full, proper sound, and articulate the consonants distinctly.

RULE 4.—Pronounce each syllable distinctly; and avoid blending the termination of one word with the beginning of another.

RULE 5.—Avoid speaking too fast, or too slow, or in an irregular manner, first slow, and then fast, or *vice versa*. By speaking fast, you will be apt to miss or half pronounce, and miscall some words, and stammer through a sentence, so that your hearers will find it difficult to understand what you are reciting. Recite no faster than you would speak ordinarily.

RULE 6.—If the subject be animated and lively, you will recite it much faster than you would one that is grave and pathetic.

RULE 7.—Be careful to emphasize properly the more important words; otherwise you will fail to convey the true meaning of the subject.

RULE 8.—Recite as if you were expressing your own thoughts and feelings; and this you should do in such a manner as to make yourself readily understood.

RULE 9.—In previously reading over the piece you have to recite, or in committing it to memory, notice the pauses or stops. They indicate the sense and relation of words. At every pause, therefore, the voice should be suspended sufficient time to mark the sense, and to take breath, so as not to destroy the sense by being obliged to make pauses wnere none are required.

RULE 10.—Let your gestures correspond with the nature of the subject; let them be under-done rather that over-done.—Practice privately as much as possible.

THE AMERICAN
TEMPERANCE SPEAKER,
No. 1.

The Power of Alcohol.

INTOXICATING liquor is deceptive in its nature, and it seems sometimes as if Satan himself had no power on earth that is doing his destroying work so effectually as this. We might almost fancy him seated upon his high and burning throne in Pandemonium, crowned with a circlet of everlasting fire, calling around him his satellites, to show their respective claims for pre-eminence by the power one possessed more than another to bring men to that burning lake. We may imagine Mammon, the meanest of all the gods, standing up and saying, " Send me : I can send men from their homes across the burning desert, or the trackless ocean, to fight and dig in the earth for yellow dust, and to harden their hearts that the cry of the widow and the fatherless shall be unheard. I will so stop up every avenue to human affection, that my victims shall stand as if made of the metal they love, and when the cold fingers of Death are feeling for their heart-strings, they shall clutch closer and closer to their hearts the bag of yellow dust, which is the only god they ever worshipped." Belial, filthiest of all the gods, next proclaims his power. Then the Destroyer asserts his claim : he holds war, pestilence, and famine in his hand, and makes men whose trade it is to deface God's image, and rank themselves in hostile array, and hurry each other, shrieking, unshrived, into another world. While all is silent, we may suppose a mighty rumbling sound, at which all hell quakes; and far in the distance is seen, borne upon the fiery tide, a monstrous being—his hair snakes, all matted with blood, his face besmeared with gore. He rises half his length, and the waves, dashing against his breast, fall back in a shower of fire. " Who art thou?" " I am an earth-born spirit; I heard your proclamation, and am come. Send me: I will turn the hand of the father against the mother, the mother against the child; the husband against his wife, the wife against her husband; the young man, in the pride of manliness, I will wrap in my cerement and wither him; the fair young girl I will make such a thing that the vilest wretch shall shrink from her in disgust. I will do more. I will so deceive them that the mother shall know that I destroyed her first-born, and yet give to me her second. The father shall know that I destroyed the pride of his hope, and yet lift the deadly draught to the lips of the second. Governors shall know how I have sapped the roots of States, and yet spread over me the robe of their protection. Legislators shall know the crime and misery I cause, but shall still shield and encourage me. In heathen lands I shall be called fire-water, spirit of the devil; but in Christendom, men shall call me 'a good creature of God.'" All hell resounds with a shout, and Satan exclaims, " Come up hither, and take a seat on the throne, till we hear thy name." As he mounts to the seat, the spirit says aloud, " My name is ALCOHOL!" and the name shall be shouted in every part of hell, and the cry be raised of, " Go forth, and the blessing of the PIT go with thee!"

J. B. GOUGH.

The Landlord.

WHAT a crafty man the landlord is,
    With his plump and smiling face;
How he chats, and smirks, and struts about
    With all becoming grace :
He welcomes you with his blandest words,
    And gives you a knowing wink,
As he hastens to his well stored bar
    To fetch you the poisonous drink.

How briskly he pokes the waning fire,
    And rubs his flabby white hands;
Or hums a tune of a merry sort,
    Or cracks a joke as he stands;
How willing he is to tell the news,
    Or an argument to start ;
And should you beg him a song to sing,
    He'll do it " with all his heart."

So long as the drink is passing free,
    The landlord's a happy man ;
He cares not a jot for your wife at home,
    Or your little ones so wan ;
He cares not though the money you spend
    Is the last that you have got;
When it is gone you may starve or die,
    For assist you he will not.

Beneath that smile on the landlord's face
    There lurks a treacherous frown ;
And deep in his heart a demon dwells,
    A demon of wide renown.
" Love of Money " is the demon's name,
    And the landlord knows right well,
For worldly gain and a life of ease
    His soul to Satan he'll sell.

I would not cherish the landlord's thoughts
  For all that the world might give;
Rather would I in a workhouse die,
  Than a wealthy landlord live;
His money is but the price of blood,
  And a curse 'twill surely bring—
A curse far worse than the curse of man,
  For aye to his soul 'twill cling!

The Angel's Visit.

UPON a bed a woman lay,
  With bloated face and tainted breath;
And by her side an infant slept,
  As calm and peaceful as in death.

The woman tossed in agony,
  For sin oppressed her guilty soul;
Though oft in drink she sought relief,
  No sleep her restless eyes control.

An angel form, enrobed in white,
  From heaven's bright portals quickly sped,
And entering that cottage home,
  Stood by the sleeping infant's bed.

Unseen he gazed with pitying eye
  Upon that mother's features wild,
Then slowly turning from the sight,
  He looked upon the babe and smiled.

O shining one! why leave your home
  Of glory and transcending bliss?
Why pass the pearly gates of heaven,
  To gaze upon a scene like this?

Come ye as messenger of love,
　To ease the erring mother's smart?
Come ye to whisper words of peace
　To her poor sin-tormented heart?

See, low the shining one bends o'er
　That tender, spotless, fragile form,
And whispers softly in its ear :
　" I come to take thee from the storm.

" This earth is all unworthy thee ;
　Thy mother's sin shall ne'er be thine ;
Come, haste away, thou fragile flower,
　To joy and happiness divine.

" Here perfect bliss thou canst not taste,
　For happiness is mixed with woe ;
There thou shalt drink celestial streams
　Which from God's throne in richness flow.

" Here storms and tempests fly around,
　And darkness often veils the way ;
There all is calm, and peace, and joy,
　With not a cloud to mar the day.

" Come then, sweet babe, nor linger here ;
　The gates of heaven are open now ;
And white-robed cherubs wait to place
　A dazzling crown upon thy brow."

The angel ceased, and plumed his wings,
　Then quickly through the air he sped ;
And when that mother turned to look,
　Behold, her infant babe was dead !

I Drink Water.

[This piece may be said by either girl or boy by changing the words in last verse.]

"I DRINK water," chirped a little bird,
"It gives me strength of wing;
And when in the sky I'm mounting high
Aloud its praise I sing."

"I drink water," said the busy bee,
As it went humming by;
"From the little well in the heather-bell
I get a good supply."

"I drink water," said the squirrel gay;
"I love the brooklet's flow;
And when I have drunk and washed my face,
A-hunting nuts I go."

"I drink water," said the pretty flower;
"It comes in sparkling dew;
And when I am weak with the summer heat
My strength it does renew."

"I drink water," said the giant oak,
"Or strong I should not be;"
And echoing notes on the calm air float
From every bush and tree.

"I drink water," said the browsing cow;
And lambkins at their play
Skip here and there, and wond'ring stare,
As the horse gives forth its neigh.

"I drink water," said a little boy;
That little boy am I;
And I hope I shall through all my life
A water-drinker be.

Temperance and Religion.

A DIALOGUE FOR TWO BOYS.

Walter. Ah, Tom! how are you? It is a long time since we met before. (Shake hands.) Which way are you going?

Tom. I am going to church to hear a sermon; will you go with me?

W. No, thank you, Tom, I am on my way to our Band of Hope meeting. I am not over partial to hearing too many sermons. I think twice on a Sunday, and once in the week nights, quite sufficient for sermons.

T. I am sorry to hear you speak so lightly about the house of God, Walter. I am afraid you have not yet experienced that new birth which Christ declares we must all experience before we can get to heaven.

W. Well, I trust in that you are mistaken, Tom. I am trying to do all I can to persuade drunkards to be teetotal, and to induce young people never to taste intoxicating drinks, and I think that is a good work.

T. No doubt it is a good work in itself. But I am afraid many teetotalers put their teetotalism in place of religion. They take a good step when they sign the pledge, but there they stop, and think their teetotalism will save them; whereas, they are as far from heaven as they were before.

W. No, no, Tom. Don't tell me that; it is opposed to common reason.

T. But, my dear friend, I can prove it from the Bible. The man who is ready for heaven is he who has believed on the Lord Jesus Christ to the saving of his soul. The words of Christ are: "He that believeth shall be saved; he that believeth not shall be damned." Now you don't mean to tell me that when a man signs the temperance pledge, that act makes him a Christian.

W. No; I am not so stupid as to think that.

T. Then you must acknowledge that religion is before teetotalism, and if you could make men religious you would not require either pledges or temperance meetings.

W. No, Tom; while acknowledging that religion is before teetotalism, I deny your last assertion altogether. I am convinced that so long as intoxicating drinks are publicly offered for sale, so long as they are used in our homes—so long will the temperance advocate be required. Until Christians become teetotalers, religion will not keep all of them from falling victims to this subtle snare of Satan. I grant you religion is the one thing needful; but how many churches have been robbed of their ministers and members, how many Sabbath-schools have had their most hopeful youth blighted and destroyed by this foul destroyer? I deny that religion will keep men from falling if they tamper with drink.

T. But I am acquainted with many good and pious men who are not teetotal.

W. That may be true. I suppose they take a little wine for their stomach's sake, and their often infirmities! But let me tell you, Tom, I think it a fearful thing for a man professing Christianity to take intoxicating drinks, even though he take them in strict moderation, while so many thousands perish yearly—each one having a soul as precious as his own. It seems to me a poor religion which will not induce a man to "deny himself" of that which has been proved beyond all doubt not only to do a man no good, but to be the source of much physical injury—even when taken in moderation. The Apostle Paul was not a man of this kind, for he says, " I will neither eat flesh, nor drink wine, nor anything whereby my brother is caused to sin."

T. That's quite true, Walter.

W. Throughout all Scripture we are warned of the danger of drink. " Wine is a mocker," says the wise man, "and whoso is deceived thereby is not wise." Look at the fearful sin Lot committed through partaking of wine. See how Herod, flushed with wine, granted a request, and seared his heart with the murder of John the Baptist. O Tom! I think if all Christians would open their eyes, they would for ever set themselves against intoxicating drink.

T. Yes, Walter, those were fearful examples you name; you seem to possess a good knowledge of Scripture on this subject.

W. If you had suffered through drink as I have, Tom, you would feel deeply about it. You know my father was once a good man ; he occupied the pulpit, and was well received as a preacher wherever he went. But alas ! he was not a teetotaler—and at length he was hurled from his high position in disgrace. But it pains me to think about it.

T. Yes, I heard all about it, and felt very sorry, for I know he was once a good man.

W. Yes, Tom, and what he has become, every professing Christian may be, if they drink intoxicating drinks. I hope you are convinced there is danger even for Christians.

T. I am afraid I have been looking at the temperance question in a wrong light. I have not been a teetotaler up to the present, nor given the subject that serious consideration I ought to have done ; but

I now see how necessary it is both for personal safety, and as an example to others.

W. I am glad to hear you speak thus. Do not for a moment think that an enlightened teetotaler puts his religion second to his teetotalism. No, no; this cannot be; but just as Christ, when about to raise Lazarus from the tomb, told the Jews to roll away the stone, in order that His voice might reach the dead man, so are we trying to roll away the black stone of intemperance from the heart of the drunkard, so that when sober and in his right mind we may point him to the Lamb of God which taketh away the sins of the world.

T. True; I see your object now; and I see, also, you are not so careless about divine things as you appeared to me at first to be. I must crave your pardon for misjudging you.

W. I trust, my dear friend, I am endeavoring to "show my faith by my works." God has in some measure blessed my feeble efforts in the good cause, and I hope you will now join with me in pulling down this stronghold of Satan.

T. I will, Walter. I have been blind in my religion; I thank you for our conversation, and must now say good-bye.

W. Good-bye, Tom. (Exit.)

Beware!

OH! ye who sip the ruddy wine,
Though like a ruby it may shine,
                    Beware!
Within the sparkling cup there lies
Unnumbered tears, and groans, and sighs,
The gnawing worm that never dies,
                    Beware!

Though great men of its virtues name,
And poets sing aloud its fame,
                    Beware!
Oh, touch it not! Its ruddy glare
Is but the lurking tempter's snare
To lead thee on to dark despair,
                    Beware!

Many, alas! have quaffed the bowl,
And soon have felt its dread control,
                    Beware!
Ah! soon the treacherous, poisoned dart
Has pierced them to the very heart,
And left a never-ceasing smart,
                    Beware!

To festive board 'tis often brought,
To waken mirth 'tis often sought,
                    Beware!
At first it tingles through the vein;
It lights the eye, and spurs the brain;
At last it leaves a throbbing pain,
                    Beware!

Many a youth, with future bright,
Has drunk the cup and felt its blight,
                    Beware!
It spares not youth or tottering age,
The thoughtless lad or hoary sage;
With all a deadly strife 'twill wage,
                    Beware!

The wise man's caution do thou take,
The ruddy, sparkling wine forsake,
                    Beware!
Pure water drink if thou wouldst be
In life unfettered, pure, and free,
Happy through all eternity,
                    Beware!

A Glass of Cold Water.

WHERE is the liquor which God the eternal brews
for all His children? Not in the simmering still,
over smoky fires choked with poisonous gases, and
surrounded with the stench of sickening odors and
rank corruptions, doth your Father in heaven pre-
pare the precious essence of life, the pure cold water.
But in the green glade and grassy dell, where the
red deer wanders and the child loves to play, there
God brews it.   And down, low down in the deepest
valleys, where the fountains murmur and rills sing;
and high upon the tall mountain tops, where the
naked granite glitters like gold in the sun; where
the storm-cloud broods and the thunder-storms crash;
and away far out on the wide wild sea, where the
hurricane howls music and the big waves roar; the
chorus swelling the march of God; there He brews

it—that beverage of life and health-giving water. And everywhere it is a thing of beauty, gleaming in the dewdrop, singing in the summer rain, shining in the ice-gem, till the leaves all seem turned to living jewels, spreading a golden veil over the setting sun, or a white gauze round the midnight moon.

Sporting in the cataract, sleeping in the glacier, dancing in the hail-shower, folding its bright snow curtains softly about the wintry world, and weaving the many-colored iris, that seraph's zone of the sky, whose warp is the rain-drop of earth, whose woof is the sunbeam of heaven, all checkered over with celestial flowers by the mystic hand of refraction.

Still always it is beautiful, that life-giving water: no poison bubbles on its brink; its foam brings not madness and murder; no blood stains its liquid glass; pale widows and starving orphans weep no burning tears in its depths; no drunken, shrieking ghost from the grave curses it in the words of eternal despair. Speak on, my friends, would you exchange it for the demon's drink, alcohol?

J. B. GOUGH.

Don't Drink, Boys.

DON'T drink, boys, don't drink,
  No matter who you be ;
When tempted, firmly answer " No !"
  And from the tempter flee.

Don't drink, boys, don't drink ;
  From you the wine cup fling ;
Beneath its ruddy glow there lurks
  The adder's venom'd sting.

Don't drink, boys, don't drink;
  'Tis but old Satan's snare
To lure you from the way that's right,
  To sadness and despair.

Don't drink, boys, don't drink;
  Though some men laud the bowl;
'Twill soon destroy your blooming health,
  And cloud your youthful soul.

Don't drink, boys, don't drink;
  If you would manly grow,
Pass by the haunts where drink is sold,
  And strong men are made low.

Don't drink, boys, don't drink;
  'Twere better you should die
While innocence dwells in your heart,
  Than in such bondage lie.

Don't drink, boys, don't drink;
  Oh, from it turn away!
And for the poor, deluded sot
  Unto your Maker pray.

The Little Soldier.

I AM a little soldier,
  And though but six years old,
Within my little breast there beats
  A heart as true as gold.

I have no gun or bay'net,
Nor sword down by my side;
Nor yet have I a prancing horse
On which to battle ride.

I have no balls or powder,
And yet, I'm proud to say,
The wicked foe I battle with
Ere long I mean to slay.

The army I belong to
Are all as brave as I,
And sooner than they'd conouered be
Will fight until they die.

Our Leader, General Temp'rance,
Oft cheers us as we go,
And tells us, if but true to him,
We're sure to slay the foe.

Our enemy is stronger
Than some of you would think;
He has a dozen different names,
But his real name is Drink.

He laughs to see such youngsters
March up and down so grand;
But never mind, he soon will find
How bravely we can stand.

Now won't you join our army?
Come, sign the pledge to-night;
We'll gladly put you through the drill,
And teach you how to fight!

The Wife's Mistake.

CHARACTERS.

George.........A carpenter	Mr. Loveall.......George's employer
Sarah.... ....George's wife	Mrs. Loveall..The wife of Mr. Loveall
Miss Lydia....President of the Women's Rights Club.	

SCENE : *Interior of a cottage. Sarah, sitting at a table.*

Sarah. How foolish young women are to get married ! They think if they can only get a husband and a house of their own they'll be the happiest beings in the world. Happy, indeed ! Much happiness there is in being a man's drudge! There may be some happiness when a woman gets a man with plenty of money, and she can pay servants to do the work; but when they're like me, have to do everything, its enough to drive any woman crazy. What with washing, cleaning, baking, mending, and one thing and another, I haven't a minute to call my own. Mrs. Goosberry has said a dozen times, " Do, my dear Sarah, come up and spend an afternoon with me," but Mrs. Goosberry doesn't know what I have to do. She's got a husband of the right sort—a man —and no mistake. He thinks nothing of going down on his knees and washing the floor, or cleaning the stove, or doing something to help his wife ; and on a Sunday morning she always goes to church, for the good man can peel the potatoes, cook the meat, and make the beds as well as his wife, and he takes a pleasure in doing it. But as for my husband, if he wants a button stitched on he says, " Here, Sarah, sew this on." It's " Do this, Sarah, do that, Sarah," until I'm completely tired out. But here he comes.

Enter George, throwing his hat on a chair, and saying—

Well, Sarah, I'm here again, you see, tired, as usual. We've had a heavy job to-day, and no mistake.

Sarah. Well, for my part, I can't understand how a man can be so tired; if he'd a woman's work to do he'd find it out. I wish I was a man.

George (laughing). Ah, ah, ah! bad tempered again, Sarah; I wish you would get over that grumbling habit. You see although I'm as tired as tired can be, I can laugh over it.

Sarah. Aye, that shows how tired you are. And as to grumbling, I should like to know who is grumbling. Its always the way with you men. If a woman tells you she's tired, she's grumbling. Here I've been slaving and slushing all day, and then because I happen to say a word, I'm grumbling.

George. Well, I'm sorry if I've hurt your feelings, but—

Sarah. Sorry, indeed! I dare say you are sorry. A great deal of sorrow you have for your wife. Don't make fun of me in that way, sir, because if you do you'll find yourself in the wrong shop. I'm not a child to be made fun of. The greatest pity is that I'm the slave of any man.

George (angrily). Well, well, that'll do. Let's have no more of that sort of talk, because, wife, I won't stand it. Is supper ready?

Sarah. Yes, there you are, tyrannical as ever. When I want to defend myself, you put me down in that way. I can't speak a word in my own defence, but you get angry, and snap at me like a dog.

George. Is supper ready, I say?

Sarah. It isn't ready. A woman can't do everything. If you was like Mr. Goosberry, you wouldn't ask, but you'd begin and get it ready. He always does, and more than that, his wife told me yesterday that he gets up first of a morning, lights the fire, and takes her a cup of tea to bed before he leaves the house. He's something like a husband, he is. I could get along with a man of that kind, who knows how to respect a woman's feelings—

George. Aye, I dare say a spooney of that sort would just suit you; but let me tell you, wife, if he's a gooseberry, I'm not. I'm not going to work for the money, and do the housework too.

Sarah. There you are—work for the money—it's always the bit of paltry money you fling at me. Don't I work, I should like to know; I work as hard as you, any day, and it's not much I eat, either. I could soon get a situation, and earn money for myself—and then I shouldn't have it flung at me so often—who earns the money?

George. You'd better get a situation, wife; the sooner the better if you are going to carry on in this way.

Sarah, Yes, that's just what you'd like me to do. I can see through it all. You want to get rid of me, after I've done for you so long, and kept things tidy and comfortable. But I'll not go—I'll stay to spite you. How can you find in your heart to tell me to go and get a situation! It's a shame, and it just shows how men respect their wives.

George. Well, wife, I'm sick and tired of this. Here I've been waiting for supper all this time, and instead of getting it ready you give me one of your usual fits of bad temper. I'm not a hard man; I can feel for you in your household difficulties, and often wish I could earn more money so that you could have a girl to help you. But I can't help you myself —at least not in the way you seem to think I ought to do. The man who will wash the floor, make the beds, and so on, is made of different stuff from me; and I think the woman that expects her husband to do these things must have a very watery idea of what a man is.

Sarah. Don't say another word. You always talk in that way. It's always me that's wrong. Whatever I say, I never get any satisfaction—but I don't believe you feel for me.

George. Well, I'm sorry, wife, to hear you say so, and as you don't seem inclined to get supper ready or make yourself agreeable, I'll go where I can be comfortable. I've had to go many a time lately because of your bad temper. Perhaps when I come back you'll be better. (Exit George, in a temper.)

Sarah. There he is, gone away to the " Red Bull " in a tantrum, just because I said I was tired. It's not because supper is not ready he goes there; it's that impudent landlady with her curls, and ribbons, and smiles, that he goes to look at. He's getting tired of both me and my company, and I think the sooner I leave him the better. It's enough to break my heart, it is, to think that after I've done so much for him, he should—like her—better—than me (bursts into tears).

Enter Miss Lydia Mandrake, dressed in the orthodox " Woman's Rights " style, and carrying a large gingham umbrella under her arm.

Miss Lydia (looking with contemptuous pity on Sarah). What, shedding tears again, Sarah! No need to tell me why—no need at all. If a woman sheds tears there's sure to be a brutish tyrant of a man at the bottom of it. The lords of creation like lording it over defenceless women. The wonder to me is why women stand it.

Sarah. I won't stand it any longer, Miss Lydia.

Miss Lydia. I should think you won't, Sarah; I

should think you won't. You've been man's slave
long enough. Ah! (brandishing her umbrella) if I
had all the men here I'd break every bone in my umbrella, that I would. To think that woman should
be the slave of man! To think that she should be so
debased and downtrodden as to wash, and clean, and
bake, and mend, and stitch buttons on, and attend to
the ungrateful animal called man. Oh! but we'll
alter this kind of thing by and by, Sarah. We'll pass
laws which shall emancipate our downtrodden sex,
and then—then the brutish male shall feel the gentle
sway of the female; then shall our tyrants fall down
on their knees and scrub the floors, clean the grates,
wash the clothes, turn the mangle; then we'll show
them who shall light the fire, make the beds, and run
the errands. That will be glorious!

Sarah. Did you never think of getting married,
Miss Lydia?

Miss Lydia. Married, Sarah! married, did you say?
Bound in the chains of slavery to a man! Never,
never! I've had many offers; the deceitful things
have tried to draw me into their embrace, but I've
resisted. They brushed their vile hair, combed out
their whiskers, twisted their moustaches, decked
themselves out in their dandyish attire, and, scented
like a druggist shop, came and fell on their knees,
told me how beautiful I was (they didn't need, Sarah,
for I always knew that), and asked me to be their
wife. Did I yield (brandishing her umbrella)?
Never, never! I despised them, I spurned them, I
bid them begone!

Sarah. Oh! if I'd only done that, Miss Lydia.

Miss Lydia. Yes, if you had, Sarah, you would
have been free. Oh, what fools most women are!
But I'm forgetting my errand. I came to ask you to

become a member of our " Women's Rights Club."
We are going to hold a meeting next week, and
draw up rules and regulations for the guidance of
those poor women who are in the abject condition
of yourself, Sarah. Will you join us ?

Sarah. Yes, Miss Lydia, I think I will.

Miss Lydia. You think you will ! There you are.
I suppose you must ask your husband first ! You
must go down on your knees, and say, " Please, husband, may 1 join the Women's Rights Club ?" You
married women have no will of your own. Be a
woman, Sarah, and say at once you'll join the club.

Sarah. Well, I'll promise you, Miss Lydia.

Miss Lydia. That's right, Sarah. Now I'll leave
you. Good evening. (Miss Lydia departs, waving
her umbrella.)

Sarah. I'm not sure whether I have done right in
telling Miss Lydia I'll join the club. I shouldn't like
George to know, at any rate ; for he'd be angry, and
no mistake. I wish he would be more agreeable,
and not go to the " Red Bull " so much. He's a good
husband after all, and not quite so bad as Miss Lydia
would make him out. No, no ; I couldn't do without
him—that I couldn't. O dear ! what must I do, for
I feel very miserable. (Sarah again weeps. A knock
at the door.) O dear, dear ! who can this be ?
Surely it can't be Miss Lydia again ; I don't want to
see her. Come in.

Enter Mrs. Loveall, neatly attired, and smiling.

Mrs. Loveall. Ah, my dear, you are weeping.
What is the matter ? Nothing serious, I hope.

Sarah. Oh ! I feel so miserable, ma'am.

Mrs. Loveall. Why miserable, my dear ? Tell me ;
perhaps I may be able to comfort you a little.

Sarah. It's George, ma'am; he's gone out angry, and I think he's gone to drink at the " Red Bull."

Mrs. Loveall. But why did he go, Sarah? George, I am sure, is not a drunken man, nor does he love the public house. My husband was only saying to-day what a clever, steady, hard-working man he is—a man who is thoughtful and intelligent, and who will soon rise to a better position than he now holds. There must be some cause, my dear, for his going to the " Red Bull."

Sarah. Well, ma'am, to speak the truth, supper wasn't ready, and I was a little vexed, for I had been working hard and was worried with family matters.

Mrs. Loveall. Ah, I see, my dear; you both got a little ruffled, and George, who I am sure is not unreasonable, went out to cool his temper, and allow yours to cool as well. Did he get his supper before he went?

Sarah. No, ma'am, I didn't get it ready for him.

Mrs. Loveall. Ah, Sarah, my dear, that was very wrong. You should never neglect to make your husband comfortable. Remember he has plenty of trouble and hard work; the life of a working man is not so easy that he can afford to lose the comforts of home. His home ought to be the spot where he can find happiness and rest; and I am sure if men's wives would only do their best to make themselves and their homes attractive, they would not go so often to the bar room.

Sarah. Well, ma'am, I think you are right. I don't think George would. It's all my fault that he went out to-night.

Mrs. Loveall. Ah, I'm glad to hear you say that, my dear. You will try and do better in the future, won't you?

Sarah. Yes, ma'am, I will, if George will only for-give me. (The door opens, and George and Mr. Loveall enter softly.) I wish he'd come, I'd ask him—

George (grasping his wife's hand). Forgive you, Sarah, of course I will. It was my fault as much as yours that we had the little brush to-night. I was tired and easily ruffled, and I didn't perhaps consider how much work you had to do at home. But I've not been to the " Red Bull." I met Mr. Loveall, and he saw I was in trouble, and he took me to his house, and there, somehow, his good wife got my trouble out of me, and she ran over to have a chat with you ; and I see she's made it all right.

Mr. Loveall. Yes, George, my wife is as good as her name ; she loves all, and is ever ready to make peace. She wasn't always so ; but you see she found out that if a woman wishes to be happy she must make her husband happy. Nothing like love at home ; it's the best thing in the world, my friends. And now, George, I'll tell you what I am going to do. My foreman has told me to-day that he's accepted a situa-tion abroad, and I'll put you in his place ; and with the extra wages you will get you can afford to let your wife have a girl to help her in her household work.

George. Oh ! thank you, sir; thank you very much. I'm sure I'll try and do my duty.

Mr. Loveall. I've no doubt of that George. I've been watching you a long time, and I know your value. There, my dear (turning to his wife), let us go and leave these two to enjoy their new-found happiness.

The door opens, and Miss Lydia, with umbrella in hand, enters.

Miss Lydia (in a loud screeching voice). The meeting begins, Sarah—

Sarah. Oh, go away, Miss Lydia. I sha'n't come to your meetings. My husband is a good, dear man, and I'm sorry I ever listened to your wicked insinuations.

Miss Lydia (raising her hands and umbrella in astonishment). What! are you turning coward? Are you going to be a slave all your life? Are you going to wash, and clean, and bake, and turn the mangle, when I told you we'd make the men do these things? Oh, what a foolish woman! Good night, Sarah; good night, Sarah, I say, and much joy may you have with the tyrants called men. (Depart Miss Lydia, flourishing her umbrella.)   .

All burst out laughing, when George begins to sing, the others joining in.

Is it True?

Boys and girls, say, is it true
Many snares are laid for you?
Of a surety can it be
Traps are set for you and me?

Yes, alas! on every hand
Great imposing temples stand,
And the gods who dwell within
Woo us to their haunts of sin.

Flaming lights and trappings gay;
Organs, merry music play;
Song and dance are daily there;
Every art to prove a snare.

These are baits to lure us in,
That we may a course begin
Which will lead us to resign
Health and peace on Bacchus' shrine.

All such places ever shun ;
For loose habits once begun
Will from bad to worse soon lead,
And the end be sad indeed.

Let your drink be water bright ;
This will ne'er your pleasures blight,
But increase your every joy,
And give peace without alloy.

Farewell to the Bottle.

[To be said slowly, distinctly, and with accompanying action. An empty bottle to stand on a table, the person reciting to address it. When near the close it will be seen the bottle is to be dashed to the floor.]

Stand there, and let me gaze at thee once more,
Ere in my wrath I hurl thee to the floor
And shatter thee ; for thou to me hast been
A tempter and a curse—a false siren—
Who led me by thy treacherous song and smile
To wretchedness and misery, and to actions vile.

When first I put thee to my youthful lip,
And took from thee a gentle, modest sip,
The liquid that thou gav'st me fired my vein,
And made my heart to dance with joy again,
It filled my brain with fancies rosy-hued,
And all along my pathway flowerets strewed ;
Till I extolled thee as some magic power
Made by the gods to brighten man's dark hour—
To drive away the sadness from his heart,
And ease the guilty conscience of its smart;
So from thy store I quaffed the nectar bright,
Till o'er my mind there fell a deadly blight.

The rosy visions which at first uprose
Dissolved in blotches on my face and nose;
My lips were cracked, my eyeballs soon were blurred,
My stomach out of order, and my tongue thick
    furred;
My head was racked with sharp and horrid pain;
And some foul demon seemed to clutch my brain;
My hands were palsied, and my eyes grew dim,
And aches and pains were felt in every limb.
But though I saw the horrors of my lot,
And knew that I was now a drivelling sot,
Such was thy potent power, I lost control,
And gave to thee my body and my soul.

With tears and sighs my friends entreated me
To break thy fetters and be rid of thee,
But from their words in rage I turned away,
And deeper quaffed thy poison day by day:
Till reason trembled on its shattered throne,
And demons jeered and mocked my piercing groan,
And I was borne, fast bound in every limb—
To where the massive walls stand high and grim,
To gloomy mad-house, reared for such as those
Who day and night with fiends like thee carouse:
There, like some ship by cruel billows tossed,
I suffered all the torments of the lost!

Thank God, my reason soon her seat regained,
And now from thy false snares I am reclaimed;
No more thy poison to my lips shall go,
No more thy venom through my veins shall flow.
I hate thee, bottle, and my hate shall last,
And from me thus thy hated presence cast;
Begone! for ever shattered mayest thou be
Unto all others, as thou art to me!

A Mournful Story.

I SAT me in my chair one night:
  The fire was all aglow,
And strong the wind went whistling by,
  And thickly fell the snow.

So cozy, snug, and warm was I,
  I quickly fell asleep ;
And visions sad flit through my brain,
  Which fairly made me weep.

I dreamed of those poor wretches who
  No home or friends could claim ;
Of those cast out upon the world
  To live by crime and shame.

I dreamed of those by drink enslaved,
  Poor victims of the bowl,
And as I dreamed a pang of grief
  Pierced to my very soul.

In dungeons dark, in madhouse high,
  How many wretches lay ;
For such as these what could I do
  But in my anguish pray ?

The wind went whistling by the door,
  And sent a rapid stream
Of chilling air right past my chair—
  Which waked me from my dream.

Then was I conscious of a sound
  Of rapping at my door ;
I started up in nervous dread,
  And stood upon the floor.

'Twas not a brisk and merry rap—
  (No dread of such had I),
It seemed as though each rat-tat was
  Accompanied by a sigh.

I mustered courage, and at length
  With care undid the door ;
Just then a mighty gust of wind
  Set up a dismal roar,

And quickly quenched the candle light
  I carried in my hand,
Which caused me such a fearful fright,
  I scarce knew how to stand.

Again the rapping sound I heard ;
  Whatever could it be ?
I through the keyhole slyly peeped,
  But nothing could I see.

Then once again I ope'd the door,
  And peered into the night,
And saw a ragged urchin stood
  Reflected in the light.

Poor little waif ! his feet were bare,
  His clothes were very old ;
How could he bear the chilling wind
  Which blew so bitter cold ?

The child of some poor, wretched sot,
  Neglected and forlorn !
And as I thought upon his lot
  My heart with grief was torn.

" Poor boy !" I said, " I pity thee ;
  Pray, wilt thou tell to me
The story of thy wretched life,
  That I may succor thee?

" Pray tell me how thy father died,
  And does thy mother drink?"
I thought I saw the urchin's eyes
  Give forth a curious blink:

He tried to speak ; his little mouth
  Was twisted all awry ;
I thought I saw the tear drops gleam,
  And heard a heavy sigh.

This long suspense I could not bear
  (My sympathies are deep) ;
I felt as though I should have burst—
  But still I could not weep.

" Come, child, be quick!—I wait thy tale !"
  Oh, sad indeed my heart!—
The boy looked up and loudly cried—
  " Done yo' want any mussels, a penny a
    quart?"

The Wreck.

A GALLANT ship sailed from the port,
  Full spread was every sail;
And ne'er a finer craft was seen
  To scud before the gale.

The captain paced the polished deck ;
  A sturdy man was he
As ever took a ship's command
  Across the briny sea.

The sailors too were brave and true,
Who knew their duty well;
And as the ship sped on its way
They thrilling yarns would tell—

Of fearful storms, hair-breadth escapes,
Of hunger, thirst, and cold;
Of shipwrecks on some foreign shore;
Of deeds both rare and bold.

A precious freight the good ship held—
Five hundred souls and more,
Besides the bales of merchandise—
A rich and goodly store.

On, on she sped right gallantly,
Her full sails gleaming white
Beneath the sun's bright rays by day,
The moon's soft beams by night.

No storm arose to check her speed,
But all was calm and bright,
With just enough of steady breeze
To keep her course aright.

She seemed to be a thing of life
Ploughing the trackless main,
Anxious to gain the distant port
That she might rest obtain.

The passengers, in merry mood,
Right gaily spent each day
In dance and mirth and jovial song;
Thus passed the time away.

The children romped about the deck,
    Brimful of life and glee;
The sailors joined them in their sports,
    And all went merrily.

" Just two days more," the captain said,
    With all a sailor's pride,
" And then our gallant little ship
    Will safe at anchor ride.

" Full twenty years I've crossed the sea,
    To many ports I've been;
But ne'er have made a swifter run,
     Or finer weather seen."

Such pleasant words were loudly cheered
    By passengers and crew;
Alas! the fate that waited them,
    How little then they knew!

The glorious day soon pass'd away,
    And from the sky shone bright,
Like myriad lamps hung out from heaven,
    The twinkling stars of night.

And while the ship ploughed o'er the deep,
    The passengers below
All met to spend a merry night,
    Their gratitude to show.

The captain's praise was loudly sung—
    While he, with beaming face,
Responded to each flattering toast
    With all becoming grace.

Swiftly the wine went round the board,
  Deeply all present drank;
Till one by one, their senses gone,
  Upon the floor they sank.

The sailors, too, upon the deck,
  Enjoyed their steaming grog;
Nor heeded they, o'er all the deep,
  The quickly gathering fog.

Still on the gallant vessel sped.
  Ah, what a fearful shock!
The cry rings out from man at helm,
  "She's struck upon a rock!"

Up rushed the captain to the deck,
  Followed by shrieks and cries;
Madly he casts his gaze around,
  Then scans the threatening skies.

"We're lost, we're lost!" he faintly said;
  "Men, women, know your fate:
See, now your vessel swiftly sinks—
  To save her 'tis too late!"

E'en while he spoke the battered ship
  With gurgling sound lurched o'er;
Then, with her full five hundred souls,
  Went down to rise no more!

My Beautiful Nose.

[A nose specially made of pasteboard and colored
should be worn during the recital of this piece.]

I ONCE had a delicate nose ;
　　An organ of beauty and grace ;
And everyone said to me then
　　How well it adorned my sweet face.
But now all its beauty has gone,
　　Ah ! gone is its rosy-tipped hue ;
An object of warning it stands,
　　With colors of purple and blue.

When walking along through the town,
　　The small boys cry, " Eh, what a nose !"
The ladies, too, step on one side,
　　Afraid of being hurt, I suppose ;
My friends (how provoking they are)
　　While taking a grasp of my hand,
Look straight at my organ of smell,
　　And tell me it's blooming quite grand.

I'm always the butt of a crowd—
　　Or rather, my nose is the butt ;
One says I have pricked it with pins ;
　　Another, I've daubed it with soot ;
One says 'tis a ball of hot fire,
　　And warns all around of their clothes :
Oh, the anguish I suffer at times,
　　Through having a flaming red nose !

If at home I chance to lie down
   And think I'll just take a short snoose,
I'm awfully bothered by flies,
   Which think they can perch where they
And when after many attempts   [choose;
   I manage to drop in a dose,
I'm suddenly startled to find
   A dozen or so on my nose.

I've tried very often to find
   Some remedy out which will hide
My nose's defects from the crowd,
   But have failed in all I have tried;
I've painted it over quite thick;
   I've dusted it well with fine flour;
But alas! none of these things availed
   When caught in a storm or a shower.

You wonder what made my nose red,
   What made its appearance so queer;
Ah! shall I confess the whole truth—
   'Tis drinking vile whiskey and beer;
Many years I've been fond of a glass
   At morning, at noon, and at night;
And this is the fruit of it all;
   Oh, dear, I'm a terrible fright!

One day a learned doctor I spied,
   And asked for his skilful advice;
He looked at my nose for a while,
   Then turned and was gone in a trice.
I was wroth at conduct so strange;
   How foolish I felt no one knows;
He might have concocted a pill
   To reduce the size of my nose!

But 'tis plain as the nose on my face
  (And that is quite plain you will say),
There's nothing will make me all right,
  But throwing the whiskey away.
Henceforward my beverage shall be
  The drink which for all freely flows;
I hope, when you see me again,
  To have a respectable nose.

The Drunkard.

HAVE you ever seen the drunkard,
  As he reels along the street,
With his hat all crushed and battered,
  Scarce a shoe upon his feet;
Hair uncombed and beard unshaven,
  Coat and trousers splashed and torn;
Mumbling, mutt'ring, stumbling, sputt'ring,
  Like a thing of reason shorn?

Have you ever seen the drunkard
  Lord it o'er his trembling wife;
Heard him threaten, without mercy,
  To crush out her wretched life;
Seen him, like a very demon,
  Hurl her senseless to the ground,
Stamping, swearing, raving, tearing,
  Worse than any savage hound?

Have you ever seen the drunkard
  When his children cried for bread,
Madly, fiercely push them from him—
  Give them brutal blows instead;

Tell them, in a tow'ring passion,
  They must go and beg or steal—
Frowning, snarling, growling, gnarling,
  Caring nothing for their weal?

Have you ever seen the drunkard
  Very early in the morn,
Sneaking from his wretched dwelling,
  Haggard, trembling, and forlorn,
Looking like a branded felon,
  As he goes along the street—
Shuffling, shaking, quailing, aching,
  Dreading any one to meet?

Have you ever seen the drunkard
  Lying on a bed of death—
Heard the fearful lamentations
  Borne upon his tainted breath;
Wishing to be free from torments,
  Yet, alas! afraid to die—
Groaning, sighing, moaning, crying,
  In his fearful agony?

Have you ever helped the drunkard
  To become a sober man?
If you have not, from this moment
  Do for him whate'er you can.
He's your brother—though so fallen—
  And his " keeper" you should be ;
Talking, coaxing, helping, loving,
  Is the work for you and me.

The Father's Example.

"I LIKE to be cozy," said Peter Brown,
  As he sat at home one night;
The curtains were drawn to keep out the cold,
  And the fire was blazing bright;
And he held in his hand a "meerschaum" grand,
  Which he smoked with great delight,
And close at his side was a glass of wine,
  Which sparkled under the light.

His little son Tommy, a smart young lad,
  Was standing beside his knee;
He looked at his sire, and smilingly said:
  "How very nice it must be
To be a big man, and sit in a chair,
  And smoke a pipe so fine!
When I am grown up I'll do just like you,
  And drink a good lot of wine."

"All right, my son Tom," his father replied,
  As he watched the curling smoke;
But Tom's mother was there, with aching heart,
  And with trembling lip she spoke:
"No, no, my dear boy, you must not say that!"
  And she took him from the room;
And the rest of the night, though all seemed right,
  Her bosom was filled with gloom.

Many years passed away; and Peter Brown
  Became a trembling old man;
His hair was white as the drifted snow,
  His face was wrinkled and wan;

And his heart was sad, for his loving wife
  Lay low in the churchyard grave;
And his only son—the once happy child—
  Was to drink a fettered slave.

The old man thought of the days that were past,
  When his home was full of joy,
When his heart was light, and the future bright
  With hopes of his darling boy.
Now those hopes were blighted—the ruddy wine
  To this child had proved a snare;
And the old man's bosom, though once so light,
  Was filled with darkest despair.

Not many months passed ere the old man died
  And was laid beside his wife;
But not too soon came the angel of death,
  For weary was he of life.
The day that they carried him to the grave
  His son in a madhouse lay—
The pipe and the bowl had darkened his soul,
  And stolen his reason away.

Band of Hope Spectacles.

A DIALOGUE FOR THREE GIRLS.

*The girls must be in walking costume. They must step
on to the platform together, and Rose, apparently dis-
pleased, must begin the dialogue at once, which must
be kept up briskly throughout.*

Rose. Well, Mary, you are a goose, and no mistake.

Mary. Why am I a goose, Rose?

R. Why are you a goose? Why, for refusing to accept the kind hospitality of our generous friend and teacher, Miss Finch.

M. But I didn't refuse to accept her hospitality.

R. Why, Mary, you did ; and I wonder how you can deny it.

M. Well, perhaps you'll explain a little more clearly.

R. Didn't she ask you to have a little refreshment?

M. Yes, and I said, " Thank you, I'll take a little."

R. Yes, I know that ; but she asked you something else.

M. What was that?

R. She said, " Will you take a little wine?" and you replied, " No, thank you," to that.

M. Of course, I know I did. But you said the same when she asked you. How can you blame me for doing what you did yourself?

R. How can I blame you? Why she asked you first, and when you refused, I couldn't say yes. If you hadn't been a goose, I tell you, we might have had a nice glass of wine with our cake.

M. But I don't see why you should be ashamed to take it, if you thought it right to do so. I refused because I believe it is wrong, foolish, and dangerous to touch either wine or any other kind of intoxicating drinks.

R. Ah, I see, that's some of the nonsense you have heard at your band of hope meetings. Well, all I can say is, I don't go with you to visit my friends again. I can't bear to see people so very particular. Besides, it's the height of rudeness to refuse anything when offered by those you are visiting.

M. I don't see it in that light, Rose.

R. Oh, of course not; you can't see anything so long as you have got your Band of Hope spectacles on—they make you blind to your own interests. You are a lot of silly geese all together.

M. Well, Rose, you say it is rude to refuse anything offered to you by those you are visiting.

R. Yes, I do; and I think I know something of manners.

M. Well, supposing Miss Finch had offered you some poison,. would it be rude to refuse that?

R. You are talking nonsense.

M. Answer my question, please.

R. Of course not. But is wine poison, you foolish girl?

M. Yes, it contains alcohol, which is one of the worst of poisons. But that is not what I was going to say. It poisons the hearts of those who take it.

R. Poisons their hearts! what folly; as if it wouldn't poison people altogether if it poisoned their hearts.

M. So it does, in time. But what I mean is this: those who drink wine or other intoxicants to excess, become brutal—their better nature is destroyed, and they sink down into mere beasts.

R. Yes, I agree with you there, when they take drink to excess; but who said anything about excess?

M. Ah! there lies the danger, Rose. Begin to take a little, and you may soon take more. The first glass is the fatal step which may, and often does, lead to utter misery and ruin. Never take the first glass, and then you can't take the second, and you will never become a drunkard.

R. That's just the way you teetotalers always talk.

M. Yes, and therein lies our wisdom.

R. But at any rate, you can't deny wine is nice to drink.

M. So 'tis said; and, therefore, the more dangerous. Most sins are nice—they are like sugar-coated pills—the sweet comes first, and the bitter after.

R. Well now, seeing that you talk so unreasonably on—

M. Not unreasonably, Rose; you can't deny that what I say is true, and—

R. Do hold your tongue, Mary, and let me speak. I declare you Band of Hope people are so very clever, and so full of argument against the drink, and you are so conceited that you won't let anybody else speak.

M. You see we've got the spectacles on.

R. There you are again; I do declare you seem ready to answer me before I have spoken. I was going to say, suppose the doctor ordered you to take wine?

M. I wouldn't take it.

R. You wouldn't take it! Oh, you silly, silly, silly girl! Do you suppose you are wiser than the doctors? If they say wine is good, it must be good.

M. Nonsense, Rose. Doctors, though generally wise and conscientious men, don't always give their patients the best of advice. This ordering of wine and other intoxicants to strengthen people who are sick and weakly is now proved to be a great piece of folly—nay, worse than folly, for not a few people die through taking them.

R. O Mary, how can you say that! Why my grandmother was ordered wine many years ago, for some disease, and she has taken it ever since; and she says when she takes a glass it seems to give her instant relief. What do you say to that?

M. Why, I say the medicine must be very slow in its cure, or else the disease is a very extraordinary one. Many people, I am sorry to say, are troubled with throat and stomach diseases, which drinking has brought on, and which, by the way they guzzle drink down, seems to be the only remedy. I'm afraid your grandmother likes the wine, and therefore thinks it does her good.

R. I hope you don't mean to insinuate that my dear old grandmother is a drunkard.

M. Not at all, Rose; though anyone seeing her red nose, would naturally suppose that she often to the bottle goes. But seriously, I think you must know that it is a most dangerous thing for young people especially to acquire a taste for these dangerous drinks. If I had thought wine was good and safe, I would not have declined to take it from Miss Finch this evening. But I am convinced it is safer to have nothing to do with it. You and I don't need it, either for our health's sake or anything else, and it is folly to talk as you do; and as to it tasting nice, there are lots of things which taste much nicer, and about which there can be no mistake.

Enter Miss Finch, in walking costume.

Miss Finch (in astonishment). Why girls, what are you doing here? It is some time since you left my house, and I expected you would have been at home before this. What is this earnest conversation about?

M. Rose has been blaming me a little for refusing the wine you offered us, and I have been defending myself.

M. F. But Rose refused, as well as yourself, and I was quite pleased.

R. Pleased, Miss Finch! I don't understand you.

M. F. Why you see, girls, I was only trying you. I had no wine to give ; but knowing that Mary was a Band of Hope girl, I thought I would see if she could withstand temptation, and I was delighted to hear her decline so kindly yet so firmly when I asked her.

R. I didn't know you were a teetotaler, Miss Finch.

M. Yes, Rose, Miss Finch no doubt wears a pair of Band of Hope spectacles.

M. F. What kind of spectacles are those, my dear?

M. (smiling). Oh, Rose said, when I was reasoning with her on the danger of taking intoxicating drinks, that I had got on a pair of Band of Hope spectacles, which made me see things in a wrong light.

M. F. I hope Rose will get a pair soon, so that she may be able to see a little clearer than she does at present. I have no doubt, Mary, you will get her a pair if she will come to one of your meetings.

M. Yes, if she will come and sign the pledge she will get a pair at once, and she will then be able to see many wonderful things.

M. F. Aye, that she will! Before I signed the pledge I was very foolish, and often argued in favor of drink ; but one evening I went to a Band of Hope meeting, and there heard what convinced me that there is death in the cup. I signed the pledge at the close of the meeting, and have never tasted intoxicating liquor of any kind since, nor do I intend to. And, Rose, every day but adds its testimony against the use of drink, and the great advantage and safety there is in total abstinence. My Band of Hope spectacles, instead of making me see in a wrong light, have revealed to me such wretchedness, misery, and poverty—such pinched and careworn faces—such hungry, ragged children—such ignorance, sin, and crime—such tears and sorrow—and all caused by drink, that I have shuddered at the sight.   But they have also revealed other sights—pictures of happiness, where peace and love and plenty reign as the results of total abstinence.   Now, Rose, which side do you think is the best—Drink or Temperance?

R. I must confess Temperance is the best.

M. F. Then you will sign the pledge?

R. Yes, that I will.

M. And you won't call me a goose any more, will you, Rosey?

R. Oh! you must forgive me, Mary; you are a dear duck.

M. F. There now, hurry home as quickly as possible, your parents will be anxious.

M. (lingering behind and addressing the audience). Now, my young friends, when Rose comes to our meeting, be sure and have ready a splendid pair of Band of Hope spectacles.

My Uncle.

WHO lives where hang three golden balls,
Where Dick's poor mother often calls,
And leaves her tippets, muffs, and shawls?
My Uncle.

Who cheers the heart with "money lent,"
When friends are cold, and all is spent,
Receiving only one per cent?
My Uncle.

Who, when I want a glass of gin,
Will take my ragged jacket in,
And keep it till I call again?

My Uncle.

Who takes my saucepan full of holes,
And shoes in want of better soles,
To raise the dust to buy the coals?

My Uncle.

Who takes the linen torn and soiled,
And cradle rocked until it's spoiled,
In short, takes all, except the child?

My Uncle.

Who, when the wretch is sunk in grief,
And none beside will yield relief,
Will aid the honest or the thief?

My Uncle.

Yet, when detection threatens law,
Who hidden stores will open draw,
That future rogues may stand in awe?

My Uncle.

Who, fortune's golden glare withdrawn,
When sycophants no longer fawn,
Takes all but honor into pawn?

My Uncle.

Who cares not what distress may bring,
If stolen from beggar or from king,
And, like the sea, takes everything?

My Uncle.

Who does all this, and think'st no sin,
And, would he yield a glass of gin,
Would take the Prince of Darkness in?
My Uncle.

Bought wisdom is the best, 'tis clear,
And since 'tis better, as more dear,
We for high prices should revere
My Uncle.

———

Which will you Choose?

WHAT would those who drink say to the man who made it his business to go from one place to another, blasting his reputation and spreading the report that he was idle, wasteful, disorderly, riotous, and a drunkard? No doubt he would be filled with rage. And yet he goes about and proclaims all this, and ten times more, by drinking every day of his life. These things are bad enough, but the drinker is not satisfied by doing evil by halves. It is not enough to render himself and those around him miserable in this world, but he is industrious in blotting out all hope of happiness in the world which is to come. There are many ways to misery, but drinking is the swiftest.

If you happen to be an honest and diligent workman, with plenty of work to do; if you possess the respect of your master and the goodwill of your fellow workmen, and have taken a fancy into your head, all at once, to get rid of your industry and your honesty, to lose the respect of your master and the good opinion of your shopmates, I will tell you how you may manage the matter in a very little time, and with little trouble—learn to drink !

If you have a strong constitution, a color on your cheek, a firm and nimble step, a regular pulse, a body free from disease, and suddenly desire to become weakly and pale, and to move along like a tottering old man, and to have a feverish pulse, and to be afflicted with half a dozen complaints at the same time, you cannot do better than listen to me. You may go the wrong way to work about the matter, you may lose time, but I will tell you how you may be sure to succeed, with great despatch—learn to drink !

If you have a comfortable and peaceful home, a cheerful fireside, with a trifle of money towards paying your rent, and have resolved to get rid of all these good things together, there are many ways of doing it, but the easiest way is to learn to drink !

If you have a suit of clothes for Sunday ; if your wife is able to dress as comfortably as her neighbors ; if your children have good clothes, and you have any inclination to see how differently you would all look if you were dressed in rags, you may easily gratify your curiosity—you have nothing more to do than to learn to drink!

If your credit is good ; if you owe nothing to any one ; if you have friends who are willing to assist you in your plans, and to stand by you in difficulties ; and you wish to run into debt, to ruin your credit for ever, and to be left without a single friend in the world, all this may be done at once, if you learn to drink !

If you have slept well ; if your mind has been at peace ; if your prospects have been cheerful ; if you have valued your Bible ; if you have taken pleasure in religious services, and at length feel a hankering after a change ; if you choose your slumbers to be broken, your mind to be disturbed, your expectations to be clouded, your Bible to be despised and religion to become a jest, then learn to drink !

If, in short, you mean to make yourself completely miserable ; to look backwards with remorse, and forwards with fear ; to live in terror, and to die in despair ; there is no surer way of doing it in the world than that of resolutely determining to learn to drink !

But now, if instead of running this wretched course, you really desire to do good and avoid evil, to live in favor with God and man, to be hopeful through time and happy in eternity; with every faculty of your body, soul, and spirit, cry aloud to the Strong for strength to resist temptation, and for grace to influence your heart, that you may never learn to drink!   Which will you choose?

––––––

What the Liquor Traffic Does.

WHAT traffic is it which, being introduced into a town, would the most neutralize the good previously effected by the churches ?

What will cause an increase of crime and social misery in proportion to its success?

What is it, the abolition of which would rob the coroner of half his fees ?

What is it, without which we should not find employment for half the jailers that are now employed ?

What is it, which the more a workingman encourages the more destitute his home becomes?

What is it, on the success of which the pawn-brokers mainly depend?

What is it that drives so many to the poorhouse ?

What is it which furnishes the greatest number of patients to asylums for the insane ?

What produces the greatest mortality among those who carry it on ?

What is it that causes so many distress warrants to be issued in poor neighborhoods?

What furnishes the greatest number of applicants to charitable institutions ?

What is it that produces the greatest number of bankrupts ?

What furnishes a resort for plunderers and bad characters ?

To what do the judges of our land ascribe the greatest proportion of criminal offences ?

What is it which, if it were introduced into some retired village, would demoralize the population now distinguished for its moral worth and frugal industry ?

It is the LIQUOR TRAFFIC.

What are you doing to suppress it ?

The Little Shoes.

IT happened on a summer's eve,
    There met in Temperance Hall
A little band of workingmen,
    Responding to a call

To come and hear the victories
    That Temperance had won ;
How fast the noble cause had grown,
    And what its friends had done.

With clapping hands and stamping feet
  Each advocate was hailed,
And not a single voice was raised
  To prove that Temperance failed.

The meeting drew towards the close,
  But still the interest grew,
And people steadily sat on
  To hear of something new.

A workingman sat near the door,
  Young, handsome, and well dressed,
His animated countenance
  Deep interest expressed.

Another workman sitting by
  Thus whispered in his ear:
" Will Turner, have you nought to tell
  Might do 'em good to hear?

" There's many here know what you were,
  And what you once could do;
Come, stand up, man, and tell 'em plain
  What made the change in you."

A buzz of voices cheered him on ;
  How could the man refuse ?
He rose at once, and stammered out
  " It was the little shoes."

You might have heard the smallest pin
  Drop down upon the floor,
So motionless the people sat,
  Expecting something more.

The speaker felt that every eye
  Was fixed upon him then,
" It was the little shoes "—he said—
  And then he paused again.

A titter ran throughout the hall;
  Will Turner heard the sound,
And in a moment stood erect
  And calmly looked around.

" Men, fathers, friends—it was in truth,
  It was the little shoes;
I've not the gift to make a speech
  This meeting to amuse;

" But I can tell a simple thing
  That happened once to me,
If you will kindly give me time
  And hear me patiently.

" It was a cold December night,
  About six months ago,
That I became a sober man,
  And I will tell you how.

" I had a wife, I had a child;
  As sweet a child and wife
As ever God in mercy gave
  To cheer a poor man's life.

" I had a home, as neat and trim
  As her dear hands could make,
And all the trouble that she took
  Was for her husband's sake.

" I let her dress in shameful rags,
　　Who loved to dress so neat;
I even let her want for shoes
　　To put upon her feet.

" Now think of that !   I blush to think
　　The villain I have been—
That I could starve both wife and child,
　　And love them less than gin !

" Oh ! when I think of what I've done,
　　Of what she has endured,
And that she lives and loves me still,
　　And that my sin is cured !

" I've said 'twas in the winter time—
　　The snow was in the street;
I knew there was no fire at home,
　　Nor yet a bit to eat ;

" I knew it—what was that to me ?
　　The drinking shop was warm ;
There I could make myself at home,
　　Nor care about the storm.

" A crowd of people filled the place ;
　　Chink, chink, the money went,
And as it trickled in the till
　　The mistress laughed content.

" Well might she laugh, while every glass
　　But added to her store,
And she was growing rich as fast
　　As we were growing poor.

" But 'twasn't that.   She had a child,
    About as old as mine;
But hers was loved and petted up,
    While mine was left to pine.

" She dressed it like a little queen,
    In warm and handsome clothes,
And then I saw her fit it on
    A pair of scarlet shoes.

" How proud they looked ! how pleased she
    That merry little thing!   [was,
The thought of my poor barefoot child
    Went through me like a sting.

" I started up, I could not stop—
    I had no will to choose—
I could not bear to see that child
    In those new scarlet shoes.

" Out on the doorstep stood my wife,
    Chilled to the very bone,
And in her trembling arms she held
    My shivering little one.

" I caught it from her arms to mine,
    I pressed it to my heart,
The touch of its small icy feet
    Struck through me like a dart.

" I hid them underneath my coat
    And then within my vest,
And there they lay and wakened up
    The father in my breast.

" They lay, and thawed the ice away—
    My heart began to beat—
Like frozen limbs roused up to life
    By glow of sudden heat.

" It was the hand of God that made
    My hardened conscience smart,
It was the little icy feet
    That walked into my heart.

" My child, thank God, is rosy now,
    My home is trim and neat,
My wife—there is not one like her
    All up and down the street.

" My story's done.   If any here
    This warning will refuse,
May God rouse him, as He roused me,
    By those two little shoes !"

                      —*Mrs. Sewell.*

Fire ! Fire !

NIGHT in New York.   What a world of meaning is hidden in that sentence.   Night in New York. Night, when poverty and misery can walk abroad unseen; when vice can wander forth without disguise; when the reveller's shout dins the ear and the blasphemer's oath makes one shudder.   Silent are the city streets: the roar of the traffic is stilled for awhile, and the footfall of the lated pedestrian echoes with startling distinctness.   What means that red glare in the sky ?   It is not near daybreak ?   No, it is the gleam and glow of fire.   See how it brightens

and then falls. Hark! others have seen the reflec-
tion, and a cry of alarm startles the midnight still
ness. " Fire ! fire !"   The cry gathers strength as it
is passed along. Fire! Fire ! Hark to the tramping
of feet!   Look, they are coming from all directions
—breathless, some hatless and coatless—as if aroused
from sleep. Now the thundering of hoofs is heard,
and the shouting of the firemen—" Hi! hi !" See
how the flames are bursting through the windows !
Hark how the rotten timber crackles ! Now they
are playing upon it with the long hose, and the deep
thud, thud of the engine sounds above the crackling
of the flames. Hark! was not that a cry for help ?
It came from that room yonder.   Quick, quick, the
ladder ! They have raised it against the window. A
sturdy fireman mounts it, his bright helmet glowing
in the blaze. Two or three strokes of his hatchet
and the sash falls in, and out streams a vast volume
of smoke, but nothing else is visible. The fireman
disappears in the aperture. The crowd hold their
breath, and the excitement becomes intense. Pre-
sently he appears again, holding the fainting form of
a woman in his arms. He has mounted the window
sill, and is preparing to descend. See, the flames
have almost reached him! Look, he is coming
down. A deafening cheer goes up as the noble fellow reaches the ground—a cheer that is worth the
winning. Rough voices shout, and great brawny
hands are stretched out to congratulate him. The
flames have reached the roof, and the rafters are
beginning to give way. Soon, with a crash and a
sputter, the roof falls, and the black and charred
skeleton of a house is all that is left on the morrow
to tell that a home has been blotted out.
Fire is a terrible enemy, but a more devouring

enemy is still going in and out amongst us. The power of the fire-demon Alcohol is not yet crippled. We have still to overcome this mighty foe. With insidious wiles he enters the homes of millions of our countrymen and ruins them. Let us give him no quarter, but whenever we see his terrible form upreared, let us shout aloud our warning cry—" Fire! fire!"

———

Mrs. Tompkins Goes to a Spelling Bee.

YES, mum, I've been to a spellin' bee as they calls 'em. I went with Missus Reynolds as keeps the chandler's shop at the corner, and a nice little body she is too, always that neat and civil as is a pleasure to be served by her. Well, I was a sittin' down enjoyin' a quiet cup of Congoo—the cup that cheers but don't intoxicate, as the poet says—when who should drop in but Mrs. Reynolds. " Oh, Mrs. Tomkins," she says, " would you like to go to a spellin' bee?" " A what, mum?" says I. " A spellin' bee. It's for the benefit of a school," she says. " Well," I says, " if it's for a deserving objects I'll go, but I never heard of such a curiosity afore. I heard about the learned pig; but a spellin' bee is an oncommon animal to be sure." " Oh," she says, " it ain't a real bee," she says. " Oh, ain't it, mum ; I suppose it's one of them tomatoms—things they move by clockwork," I says. " No, mum," she says; " it's a competition—a spellin' competition." "Whatever do they call it a bee for," I says, "if it isn't one?" " I don't know," she says, "unless it means industry. It's ladies and gentlemen spellin' for prizes." "Oh," I says, "there's a good many as does that, but them that spells most shouldn't get anything if I had my way." "It's spellin' words out of a dickshunary," she says. "Oh," I says, "it wouldn't do for me; I never was reckoned very clever at spellin' at school, and I've forgotten a'most all that I learnt except the tingle of the cane when they punished me." "Oh," she says, "you won't have to spell anything; we only look on at the others." "Oh," I says, "if that's it, I'm all right." So it was agreed on as how she was to call for me, and we were to go into the reserved seats so as to have a good chance of hearing. Well, she came punctual, and we started together. When we got there, the people were going in like a pantomine. There was such a lot of nicely dressed ladies on the platform that I began to think as how it was a milliner's exhibition. A nice old gentleman took the chair, and made a speech about Dr. Johnson, and Webster, and all the great men as wrote dickshunaries. He told us how we ought to study our mother tongue. "Oh," I says to Mrs. Reynolds, "Tomkins' mother was an Irish woman; if he'd have learnt her langwidge he wouldn't have been much better off, I reckon." After the chairman's speech there was some singing, and then the interrorgaiters as they calls him, comes to the front of the platform, and began to ask the ladies to spell a lot of words. As my grandmother used to say, they was regular jawbreakers. "Spell ' matrimony,' " he says to one very sour-faced looking lady with corkscrew curls and spectacles. "I dessay that's what she's been spellin' for a long time," I says. "Hush!" says Mrs. Reynolds, "she'll hear you." "Spell ' sheenong,' " he says to a young lady with a great cottage loaf at the

back of her head. She didn't spell it right, and so
she had to go down. Oh, didn't the young men
giggle at her, that's all. " Spell ' vinegar,' " he says
to a very sour looking old man as looked like a walking dickshunary; but he didn't spell it right, and when
the people laughed at him he looked so savage as I
thought he was going to give some on 'em a tap with
his walking stick. " Spell ' valentine,' " says the interrorgaiters to a young lady. But, la ! she giggled,
so it set all the people off, and it was a long time before she could say anything at all. But she spelt it
right after all. " She was thinking about it," I says
to Mrs. Reynolds, " while she was laughin'; you
mark my words, she's a knowing young puss."
Then they asked a young man to spell a word as
sounded foreign to me. " Oh," says he, " there's
two ways of spellin' that word ; which way shall I
spell it ?" " Both," says the interrorgaiters. He tried
to spell it two different ways. " Both wrong," says
the gentleman with the book. Whatever they called
him that funny name about gaiters for I can't think.
He had a beautiful pair of black trousers on, and no
leggings of any sort. Perhaps his father used to
wear gaiters. I thought of asking Mrs. Reynolds
once or twice, only I didn't like to look ignorant.
The chairman said in order to give variety to the
entertainment there would be. some music. Then
a young gal, with long curls, come and sat herself
down to the piannerfortee, and punished the instru-
ment, as Tomkins calls it. " Whatever is she trying
to play ?" I whispers to Mrs. Reynolds. " It's a
galop," she says. " Oh, is it; it looks like it." For
the young gal was a shaking her head and banging
into that piannerfortee in a very violent manner.
After that was over (and I wasn't sorry when it was)

a tall young lady in blue silk came forward and sang something about wanting a bird to come and live with her. "La," I says to Mrs. Reynolds; "she's only got to purwide a cage, and some seed, and some clean sand, and to give it plenty of water; but if she was to leave the door of the cage open and begin to make the awful noise as she's making now, the bird would be off in a jiff." But, la! the peope clapped and hollered oncore like mad. Then a young man sang a very sorrowful sort of piece about a young lady as he kept asking to meet him once again. And then there was more spellin' by the ladies and gentlemen. There was only three prizes, and the people got very tired before it was over. My opinion is as how spellin' bees may be all very well, but I don't see the use of a lot of people exposin' their ignorance on a platform. Why don't they go to an evenin' school? I'd much rather go to school if I was ever so old, than be stared at on a platform. What's the School Board doin' I want to know? If they can't teach people to spell so as they sha'n't look ridiculous in company, what's the good on 'em? But the words they ask you to spell are no manner of use to honest people. Whenever I write a letter I always put P. S.—Please excuse the spellin'. I think I shall put in my postscriptions for the future—" Please excuse the spellin' bee."

The Auction.

WILL you walk into the auction, for the sale is just
     begun,
And bid and buy, my masters all, before the lots are
     done?
Such wondrous curiosities were ne'er exposed to
     view,
So I pray you pay attention while I read th' in-
     vent'ry through.
                         Will you walk into the auction?

Lot I.—Some dirty dishes, which have once been
     edged with blue,
But, alas! the rims are broken, and they let the
     water through;
A broken knife, a one-pronged fork, and half a
     wooden spoon,
And a little penny whistle, which has never played a
     tune.
                         Will you, etc.

Lot II.—A crazy fiddle, without finger-board or peg;
'Twas broken at the Fox and Goose, when
     " Scraper" broke his leg;
The fiddle-bag and fiddle-stick are with it, I declare,
But the one is full of moth-holes, and the other has
     no hair.
                         Will you, etc.

Lot III.—An old oak table, which has once been
     neat and small,
But having lost a pair of legs, it rests against the
     wall;

The top is split, the drawers are gone, its leaves
    have dropped away,
And it has not felt the weight of food for six months
    and a day.
            Will you, etc.

Lot IV.—The shadow of a chair, whose back and
    seat are fled ;
The latter Jenny burnt, because the former broke
    her head;
And now they've tied its crazy joints with cords of
    hempen string,
And it creaks when it is sat upon, just like a living
    thing.
            Will you, etc.

Lot V.—A truss of barley straw, and two small
    pokes of chaff,
Which have served for bed and pillows just five
    years and a half;
Two sheets of homespun matting, of the very coarsest
    grain,
And a piece of ragged carpeting, which was the
    counterpane.
            Will you, etc.

Lot VI.—A corner cupboard, with the things con-
    tain'd therein—
A spoutless teapot and a cup, both well perfumed
    with gin—
A broken bottle and a glass—a pipe without a
    head—
And a dirty, empty meal bag, where two mice are
    lying dead.
            Will you, etc.

Lot VII.—One old bottle neck, bedaubed with
     grease so thick,
Which formed when they'd a candle, a convenient
     candlestick;
Also, an old tin kettle, without handle or a spout,
And a pan, of which a neighbor's child had drumm'd
     the bottom out.
                    Will you, etc.

Lot VIII.—A het'rogeneous heap of bits of odds
     and ends,
Which you may purchase very cheap as presents for
     your friends;
Also, some locomotive rags, which move with per-
     fect ease,
Like the little coach we read of, that was drawn by
     little fleas.
                    Will you, etc.

Come, walk into the auction, for my catalogue is
     through,
Yet I have just one word to say, before I bid adieu.
These lots are all produced by Drink—which you'll
     do well to shun,
Before your health and substance too, are "going,
     going—GONE!"

———

The Curious Dose.

AN officer in quarters lay
     At Dublin—I may say
His case was fever, raging, burning—
     He took to his bed,
     With fiery eyes and aching head,
And tossed as if on glowing cinders turning.

The doctor came ('twas very needful)—
And he displayed his skill most heedful ;
He wrote for pills and draughts to drive
The demon out—dead or alive ;
And ordered, as he might be worse,
A steady, careful, good old nurse ;
And quickly to the patient came—
As recommended—the old dame.

She poured the draught into a cup,
And soon the sick man drank it up ;
The box of pills with care she placed
Where various things the mantel graced,
Because two hours must pass away,
To let the potion have fair play.

That time elapsed, Nurse made all speed
The patient with the pills to feed—
She ope'd the box, and gave him two,
He gulped them down without ado ;
Two more, and then two more must follow,
These rather stuck within his swallow ;
" Good Nurse, some drink !" He drank, and then
Boldly attacked the pills again.
Two more went down, and then two more,
Which made the number half-a-score.

" More drink ! so many is provoking—
My throat is full—I'm almost choking."
" Arrah, my jewel, let me tell
You these will shortly make you well."

Two more he took : " I prithee, say,
    Good Nurse, how many there remains ? "
" Two, four, five, seven, nine, ten, twelve—aye,

By Shelah, good St. Patrick's cousin,
  The box contains—
Exact another dozen!"

"A dozen more!" the sick man cries
(Trembling with fever and surprise)
" I thought apothecaries vended
By retail till their patients mended ;
This sells the poison by wholesale!"

This boisterous gale
Of angry passion o'er,
She coaxed him to get down two more,
And thus at length he swallowed twenty-four!
Worn with fatigue, sometime he lay,
To pain and angry thoughts a prey,
But soon his agony increased,
  For, lo! the pills lay undigested
  Hard at his stomach, there they rested,
And filled with dreadful pain his breast.

The doctor must be called—he came ;   [ders ;
  Inquired each symptom—shrugged his shoul-
He, apprehensive for his fame,
  And for the patient one or two beholders—
"Did you administer the draught ?" " Oh, yes !"
"The pills?" " 'Tis they that have caused all this,"
Exclaims the officer. " Did you suppose
I was a horse, that you sent such a dose ?
I've four-and-twenty bullets lying
In my stomach—and I'm dying."
"Bullets!" repeats the doctor, with surprise,
  "Sir, I'm a man of peace, and every pill
  I sent was meant to cure—not to kill.
Besides I sent but two," he straight replies.
" I've swallowed twenty-four !" the sick man cries.

A squinting servant of the house stood by,
And toward the shelf she cast an eye :
She ope'd the doctor's box, and there
The pills both snug and safe appear.
Another box upon the shelf remained
    Empty. " Why, Nurse," she squalls,
    And at the doctor like a fury bawls,
" This box, now empty, once contained
    What the poor gentleman has taken—
Were he an ostrich, or the prince of gluttons,
    You'd scarcely save his bacon,
        For, sans leaven,
        You have given
Him two dozen round shirt buttons!

A Call for Help.

MR. CHAIRMAN, Ladies, and Gentlemen—I believe
intemperance to be a great curse to the land in which
we live, and an enemy both to God and man. I
know, sir, persons are to be found (perhaps there are
some present) who ask: " What harm is there in
just taking, now and then, a glass of beer or a drop
of brandy?" I reply : '' Afterwards it biteth like a
serpent and stingeth like an adder." Do any of you
ask: " What harm does drink do?" If so, allow me
to say that my experience, limited as it is on account of my youth, leads me to think that it does
nothing but harm.

I remember, sir, a fable of a serpent being surrounded by fire, and in this critical position request-
ing a man to set it free. This he agreed to do if the
serpent would promise not to sting him. The ser-

pent readily consented. When set free, however, it instantly stung its deliverer. Upon the man accusing the serpent of ingratitude, and reminding it of its promise, it simply replied: " Ah, sir, it's my nature to sting!" Now, sir, I firmly believe that the very tendency of drink is to injure and destroy.

Should any doubt, I would ask, in the eloquent language of a living writer: " Has it not led thousands to the jails, and hundreds to the scaffold? Has it not made women widows while their husbands lived, and children orphans ere their parents died? Has it not sent brothers far across the sea, and hung with chains the limbs that once were free? What has it not done? What dismal woe has it not produced? What soft affection has it not massacred? With what virtuous blood are not its murderous hands besmeared? It is the devil's truest weapon, the serpent's subtlest poison. Its pathway is paved with broken hearts and strewn with withered hopes. It leads from contentment to distress, from distress to want, from want to vice, from vice to crime, from crime to punishment, from punishment to disease, from disease to death, from death to the grave, from the grave to the judgment, and from the judgment to damnation."

If this be true, ladies and gentlemen, what ought we to do? What? Why, we ought all to do everything we can to slay the great Philistine.

> Through the land there is stalking a giant-like foe,
> Who spreads in his track sin, sorrow, and woe ;
> Who smites down all classes—the rich and the poor,
> The aged and the young, lie faint at his door.
> He enters the home of the hard-working man,
> And robs him of every possession he can ;
> His wife and his children he fills with despair,
> And the spot once so bright is beclouded with care.

But, sir, the time is coming when the blessings of total abstinence shall fill the dwelling-place of man. Much has yet to be done before the long-wished and prayed-for day arrives, but come it will, if we do our duty. I earnestly appeal to you for assistance Are you followers of Him " Who for our sakes became poor, that we through His poverty might become rich?" Then I especially call to you for help. It ought to be, it must be, your highest ambition to remove everything that impedes the progress of truth. If the wilderness and the solitary places are to be made glad, if the desert is to blossom as the rose, you must help us. The late Dr. Guthrie once said : " Until the Church of God will face manfully and Christianly the great drink curse, no great aggression will be made upon the sorrows or the miseries of the people." Assist us then by your earnest efforts and your faithful prayers. Your aim being good and your motives pure, success shall be your reward. Then arise, ye people of God, in the name of your Master and in the cause of humanity, and, moved by Christian zeal and brotherly feeling, take in your hand the battle-axe of Temperance, and rest not satisfied until you have slain the enemy !

What Doest Thou Here?

It is Saturday night, and the week is near past,
　All its toils and its burdens are o'er,
And the smile of content shineth bright on his face
　As the cottager closes his door.
'Tis eleven o'clock ; it is time to be gone,
　For the morn of the Sabbath draws near—
There's a fire in thine eye, there's a fiend in thy brain ;
　O, drunkard ! what doest thou here?

Perchance a fond wife, with a sad broken heart,
　　Is watching all weary and worn,
With a tear in her eye, with despair in her breast,
　　And a spirit all tattered and torn.
Oh, think, it is her whom you vow'd to adore,
　　To nourish, protect, and to cheer;
Then why hast thou left her in anguish to mourn?
　　O, drunkard! what doest thou here?

And hast thou no children to need thy strong arm,
　　Nor wand'rer for thee to reprove?
No fond ones to climb up thy fatherly knees,
　　And clasp thee like clusters of love?
No son that is rip'ning for good or for ill,
　　And needing thy counsel and care,
Or daughter ensnared by the smiles of deceit?
　　O, drunkard! what doest thou here?

There's a tread in the street of some little one's feet,
　　All naked and bleeding and sore;
There's a shivering body all purple with cold—
　　Ah, me! it is hard to be poor!
But her mother has nothing to give her to eat,
　　For her cupboard is naked and bare;
And her father sits long o'er his glasses of ale,
　　O, drunkard! what doest thou here?

It is Saturday night, 'tis eleven o'clock,
　　And the morn of the Sabbath draws near;
Then haste for your life, and be gone to your home,
　　'Tis the time of refreshing and prayer.
Go, gather your lov'd ones and cry to your God
　　To give you repentance sincere;
He will not reproach thee, He will not condemn,
　　Nor ask thee, What doest thou here?

The Discontented Pendulum.

AN old clock that had stood for fifty years in a farmer's kitchen, without giving its owner any cause of complaint, early one summer's morning, before the family was stirring, suddenly stopped.

Upon this the dial-plate (if we may credit the fable) changed countenance with alarm ; the hands made a vain effort to continue their course ; the wheels remained motionless with surprise ; the weights hung speechless ; each member felt disposed to lay the blame on the others. At length the dial instituted a formal inquiry as to the cause of the stagnation, when hands, wheels, weights, with one voice protested their innocence. But now a faint tick was heard below from the pendulum, who thus spoke : " I confess myself to be the sole cause of the present stoppage ; and I am willing, for the general satisfaction, to assign my reasons—the truth is, that I am tired of ticking." Upon hearing this, the old clock became so enraged that it was on the very point of striking.

" Lazy wire !" exclaimed the dial-plate, holding up its hands.

" Very good !" replied the pendulum. " It is vastly easy for you, Mistress Dial, who have always, as everybody knows, set yourself up above me—it is vastly easy for you, I say, to accuse other people of laziness ! You who have had nothing to do all the days of your life but to stare people in the face, and to amuse yourself by watching all that goes on in the kitchen. Think, I beseech you, how you would like to be shut up for life in this dark closet, and to wag backwards and forwards, year after year, as I do. I am really tired of my life ; and, if you wish, I'll tell you how I took this disgust at my employment. I happened this morning to be calculating how many times I should have to tick in the course only of the next twenty-four hours ; perhaps some of you above there can give me the exact sum ?"

The minute-hand, being quick at figures, instantly replied : " Eighty-six thousand four hundred times."

" Exactly so," replied the pendulum. " Well, I appeal to you all, if the very thought of this was not enough to fatigue one ; and when I began to multiply the strokes of one day by those of months and years, really it is no wonder if I felt discouraged at the prospect ; so, after a great deal of reasoning and hesitation, thinks I to myself—I'll stop."

The dial could scarcely keep its countenance during this harangue, but resuming its gravity, thus replied : "Dear Mr. Pendulum, I am really astonished that such a useful, industrious person as yourself should have been overcome by this sudden action. It is true you have done a great deal of work in your time, so have we all, and are likely to do ; which, although it may fatigue us to think of, the question is, whether it will fatigue us to do. Would you now do me the favor to give half-a-dozen strokes, to illustrate my argument?"

The pendulum complied, and ticked six times at its usual pace.

" Now,' resumed the dial, " may I be allowed to inquire, if that exertion was at all fatiguing or disagreeable to you ?"

" Not in the least," replied the pendulum ; " it is not of six strokes that I complain, nor of sixty, but of millions."

" Very good," replied the dial ; " but recollect that though you may think of a million strokes in an instant, you are required to execute but one ; and that, however often you may hereafter have to swing, a moment will always be given you to swing in."

" That consideration staggers me, I confess," said the pendulum.

" Then I hope," resumed the dial-plate, " we shall all immediately return to our duty ; for the maids will lie in bed till noon, if we stand idling thus."

Upon this, the weights, who had never been accused of light conduct, used all their influence in urging him to proceed ; when, as with one consent, the wheels began to turn, the hands began to move, the pendulum began to swing, and to its credit ticked as loud as ever ; while a red beam of the rising sun that streamed through a hole in the kitchen shutter, shining full upon the dial-plate, it brightened up as if nothing had been the matter.

When the farmer came down to breakfast that morning, upon looking at the clock, he declared that his watch had gained half-an-hour in the night.

MORAL.

In looking forward to future life, let us recollect that we have not to sustain all its toil, to endure all its sufferings, or to encounter all its crosses at once. One moment comes laden with its own little burdens, then flies, and is succeeded by another no heavier than the last ; if one could be borne, so can another and another. Even in looking forward to a single day, the spirit may sometimes faint from an anticipation of the duties, the labors, the trials to temper and patience that may be expected. Now this is unjustly laying the burden of many thousand moments upon one. Let any one resolve always to do right now,

leaving then to do as it can; and if he were to live
to the age of Methuselah, he would never do wrong.

It seems easier to do right to-morrow than to-day,
merely because we forget that when to-morrow
comes, then will be now; thus life passes with many
in resolutions for the future which the present never
fulfils.

It is not thus with those who, " by patient continu-
ance in well-doing, seek for glory, honor, and immortality "—day by day, minute by minute, they execute the appointed task to which the requisite
measure of time and strength is proportioned; and
thus, having worked while it was called day, they at
length rest from their labors, and their " works follow them."

Let us, then, " whatever our hands find to do, do it
with all our might," recollecting that now is the
proper and " accepted time."

Down in the Mire.

Down in the slush and mud of the street,
Kick'd on one side by the passengers' feet,
Hat batter'd in, and eyes flashing fire,
Headlong the drunkard falls down in the mire.

'Bus drivers shout, as he staggers along,
Yelling the chorus of some filthy song,
With his hoarse voice rising higher and higher;
But now he has fallen down into the mire.

Boys selling " box o' lights " yell at his heels,
Stones fly fast at him as onward he reels,
A crowd gathers round, and ask, " Is it fire?"
" No, it's only a drunken man down in the mire."

Ladies shrink from him and shudder with fear,
Lest the poor drunkard should stagger too near,
Drawing up closer their silken attire,
Lest he should spatter their clothing with mire.

Foot-passenger, stop, ere you pass on your way ;
Don't tell me you're awfully busy to-day ;
You have put down your name to build a church
    spire—
Here's a broken-down temple down in the mire.

Ruddy-cheek'd boy, on your way to the school,
Cramming your head with hard science by rule,
Don't think that book-learning is all you require—
Here's a lesson for you, my boy, down in the mire.

Don't open your blue eyes so wide on me now !
Don't curl up your lip and wrinkle your brow !
He once was a schoolboy with heart full of fire,
But now he lies helpless down in the mire.

Young maiden, with curls like bright threads of pure
    gold—
Forgive me, fair maiden, if I am too bold ;
You have health, you have beauty, and all you
    desire ;
Just look for one moment down in the mire.

You have lovers in plenty, who sigh at your feet,
But there's one, and one only, whose whisper is
    sweet ;
It is right you should love him ; but, lady, come
    nigher—
He was somebody's lover once—that man in the
    mire.

Little girl, little girl, singing blithely with glee,
Just stay for one moment and listen to me:
When you bring papa's slippers to warm at the fire,
Think of somebody's father, who's down in the mire.

Yes, somebody's father's down in the street,
Kick'd on one side by the passengers' feet,
Hat batter'd in, and eyes flashing fire,
Yelling out curses while down in the mire.

Will nobody help him? will nobody save
This poor stranded wreck on life's troubled wave?
Yes, yes! we will struggle to lift him up higher,
Though we have to go down deep into the mire.

An Honest Publican's Advertisement.

FRIENDS AND NEIGHBORS—Grateful for the liberal
encouragement received from you, and having sup-
plied my shop and tavern with a new and ample
stock of choice wines, spirits, and malt liquors, I
thankfully inform you that I continue to make
drunkards, paupers, and beggars, for the sober, industrious, and respectable community to support.
My liquors may excite you to riot, robbery, and
blood, and will certainly diminish your comforts,
augment your expenses, and shorten your lives. I
confidently recommend them as sure to multiply
fatal accidents and distressing diseases, and likely to
render them incurable. They will agreeably deprive
some of life, some of reason, many of character, and
all of peace—will make fathers fiends, wives widows,
mothers cruel, children orphans, and all poor. I will
train the young to ignorance, dissipation, infidelity,

lewdness, and every vice—corrupt the ministers of religion, obstruct the gospel, defile the church, and cause as much temporal and eternal death as I can.

I will thus "accommodate the public," it may be at the cost of my never-dying soul. I have a family to support—the trade pays—and the public encourage it. I have a character from my minister, and a license from the magistrate ; my traffic is lawful ; Christians countenance it ; and if I do not bring these evils upon you somebody else will. I know the Bible says, " Thou shalt not kill,"—pronounces a " woe unto him that giveth his neighbor drink," and enjoins me not to . " put a stumbling-block in a brother's way." I also read that " no drunkard shall inherit the kingdom of God," and I cannot expect the drunkard-maker, without repentance, to share a better fate ; but I wish a lazy living, and have deliberately resolved to gather the wages of iniquity, and fatten on the ruin of my species. I shall therefore carry on my trade with energy, and do my best to diminish the wealth of the nation, impair the health of the people, and endanger the safety of the state. As my traffic flourishes in proportion to your ignorance and sensuality, I will do my utmost to prevent your intellectual elevation, moral purity, social happiness, and eternal welfare. Should you doubt my ability, I refer you to the pawn-shop, the poor-house, the police-office, the hospital, the jail, and the gallows, where so many of my customers have gone. The sight of them will satisfy you that I do what I promise.

N.B.—I teach old and young to drink, and charge only for the materials ; a very few lessons will be sufficient.

The Death of the Reveller.

THE lights were gleaming and the feast was spread,
And at the table sat the boisterous guests,
Shouting and singing snatches of coarse songs.
The giver of the feast was an old man,
Grown old in sin, and harden'd more and more,
Till age found him, 'mid the boisterous crew,
A guide and prompter into any path
That led away from virtue or from truth.
His snow-white hair upon his shoulders fell
In twining ringlets ; and his silver beard,
Grizzled with age, clung to his hollow cheeks ;
And on his brow the plough of time had made
Deep furrows ; and his eyes were growing dim.
But still his hollow voice rang on the night,
And his eye glisten'd at the obscene jests
Of his companions, and his skinny hands
Beat on each other with a hollow sound
At the rude singing of the rabble crew.
It was an awful sight to see him there,
So old and wither'd, yet so wildly gay ;
So like a patriarch, yet so like a fiend.
The ruddy wine was pour'd incessantly ;
And as the brimming goblets pass'd along,
The old man chuckled, and his eyes grew bright.
He seized a flagon in his trembling hands,
And held it to his lips, and shriek'd aloud,
The while it ran like blood upon his beard,
And trickled to the floor.   At each fresh draught
New vigor seem'd to nerve his aged limbs,
And he sat more erect, and lifted up
His trembling voice and sang an ancient song.
The vaulted roof re-echo'd with the shouts
Of the mad revellers when the song was o'er,
And eagerly they call'd out, " Sing again !"

The old man took another draught of wine,
And, smiling, once again essay'd to sing.
It was a love-song—a sweet, simple thing—
A song he oft had sung in his fresh youth,
When his young heart was gay as any bird's,
And life was like a glorious dream of flowers.
His trembling voice grew stronger as he sang,
And his hard features soften'd, and a smile
Play'd o'er his face, and in his glistening eye
A tear-drop stood.   His inmost soul was stirr'd
With thoughts of other days, and his harsh voice
Grew soft as woman's, and his radiant face
Beam'd with the light of tender memories.
But suddenly his cheek turn'd deadly pale,
And he fell backward, with his long lean hand
Press'd to his side, as if with sudden pain.
The guests, alarm'd, ran quickly to his aid,
And raised him up, and press'd a brimming cup
Against his lips.   But, with a gesture, he
Put it away, and lifting up his head,
Spake in a solemn voice, unlike his own,
While the dazed revellers stood silent by:

    " Nay, tempt me not again !
I will not touch the wine-cup in this hour :
Too often have I felt its deadly power ;
    And I would clear my brain
In these last trembling moments, for I feel
Death's icy hand across my temples steal.

    " Nay, do not smile at me
And mock me with false hope of many days :
My time has come : this is death's filmy haze
    That will not let me see
Your faces round me, though the lamps are bright
And the wine glitters in the sparkling light.

" To die in such a place!
I who once knelt beside my mother's knee
To say my evening prayer.   And must it be
  That I may ne'er retrace
The pathway of my life, lest haply I   ·
Might do one deed of good before I die?

" And must I die to-night,
With the still echoing songs to mar my peace,
To bid all thoughts of heavenly subjects cease?
  Ere the sun's golden light
Streams through the windows of this awful place,
Death will have stamp'd his impress on my face.

" Oh! listen to my voice,
Ye, who have often shouted with delight
At my rude jesting, listen now to-night.
  Ye, who in youth rejoice,
Be warn'd by me, and stay while yet 'tis time,
Ere your young souls get harden'd unto crime.

" Oh! shun the wine-cup now!—
Now, while the light of youth is in your eye;
While hope weaves golden colors in your sky;
  Ere yet upon your brow
The frosts of winter fall, and time's rough share
Plough, deep and lasting, bitter furrows there.

" I have been wont to sneer
At holy themes, and laugh at those who trod
The path of virtue and look'd up to God
  With holy, reverent fear.
But now I would give worlds if I could pray
The prayer I would repeat at close of day.

"Raise my head higher now—
Open the windows, let me have more air—
I cannot breathe!—why do you wildly stare?
This cold sweat on my brow
Is death, I know. I faint—I reel—I fall!
Mind my last words. Ha! may God save you all."

His head fell back; and they who watch'd him die
Stood gazing at each other for awhile;
And then with soft, slow steps they one by one
Crept silently away. The banquet-hall
Is silent and deserted, and the walls
No longer echo to the revellers' mirth.
There is a solemn stillness in the place,
As if the ghost of the departed hours
Had found a refuge there. The owlet screams
About the windows; and the moonlight falls
Upon the empty board; and all is still.

———

The Vagrants.

CHARACTERS:

A landlord, seated in his bar;
A vagrant, who enters with his fiddle and dog.

Vagrant. We are two travellers, Roger and I.
　　Roger's my dog, and if you please
You'll let us come in by your stove to dry,
　　For the rain and sleet to my garments freeze.
The rogue is growing a little old;
　　Five years we've tramped through wind and
　　　　weather,
And slept out-doors when nights were cold,
　　And ate and drank—and starved together.

We've learned what comfort is, I tell you ,
    A bed on the floor, a bit of rosin,
A fire to thaw our thumbs (poor fellow ?
    The paw he holds up there's been frozen),
Plenty of cat-gut for my fiddle
    (This out-door business is bad for strings),
Then a few nice buckwheats hot from the griddle,
    And Roger and I set up for kings !

Landlord. Will you have a drink ?
V. No, thank you, sir, I never drink ;
    Roger and I are exceedingly moral,
Ain't we, Roger ?
L. 'Twill warm you, I think.
V. Well, something hot, then ; we won't quarrel.
        [The landlord pours a glass for him.]

The truth is, sir, now I reflect,
    I've been so sadly given to grog,
I wonder I've not lost the respect
    (Here's to you, sir !) even of my dog.   [Drinks.]
But he sticks by me, through thick and thin ;
    And this old coat, with its empty pockets,
And rags that smell of tobacco and gin,
    He'll follow while he has eyes in his sockets.
There isn't another creature living
    Would do it, and prove, through every disaster,
So fond, so faithful, and so forgiving
    To such a miserable thankless master !
We'll have some music, sir, if you are willing.

    [He plays a tune ; any sweet, old tune that will
touch a chord in men's hearts will do.]

    L. Are you not tired of this kind of life ? Why
don't you reform ?
    V. Why not reform ? That's easily said ;
    But I've gone through such wretched treatment ;

Sometimes forgetting the taste of bread,
  And scarce remembering what meat meant,
That my old stomach's past reform ;
  And there are times when, mad with thinking,
I'd sell out heaven for something warm
  To prop a horrible inward sinking.
Is there a way to forget to think ?
  At your age, sir, home, fortune, friends,
A dear girl's love—but I took to drink—
  The same old story : you know how it ends.
If you could have seen these classic features—
  You needn't laugh, sir ; they were not then
Such a burning libel on God's creatures :
  I was one of your handsome men !
If you had seen her, so fair and young,
  Whose head was happy on this breast !
If you could have heard the songs I sung
  When the wine went round, you wouldn't have
    guessed
That ever I, sir, should be straying
  From door to door, with fiddle and dog,
Ragged and penniless, and playing
  To you to-night for a glass of grog !
L. What became of her you loved ?
V. She's married since—a parson's wife ;
  'Twas better for her that we should part—
Better the soberest, prosiest life
  Than a blasted home and a broken heart.
L. Have you ever met her since?
V. I have seen her once ; I was weak and spent
  On the dusty road ; a carriage stopped :
But little she dreamt as on she went,
  Who kissed the coin that her fingers dropped !
You've set me talking, sir ; I'm sorry ;
  It makes me wild to think of the change !

What do you care for a beggar's story?
　Is it amusing? you find it strange?
I had a mother so proud of me!
　'Twas well she died before——Do you know
If the happy spirits in heaven can see
　The ruin and wretchedness here below?
Another glass, and strong, to deaden
　This pain; then Roger and I will start.
I wonder has he such a lumpish, leaden,
　Aching thing, in place of a heart?　　[Drinks.]
L. Well, my poor fellow, you do not lead a very gay
　　life, I think.
V. Not a very gay life to lead, you think;
　But soon we'll go where lodgings are free,
And the lodgers need neither victuals nor drink—
　The sooner the better for Roger and me.

Only a Woman Drunk.

A CROWD in the busy street,
　A block in the bustling way,
A pause for the weary feet,
　That scarcely have time to stay.
" What is the matter? say!
　Some one to earth has sunk,
Why do they stop the way?
　It's only a woman drunk."

Only a woman drunk!
　Look at her as she lies,
With her face all mud and dirt,
　And that wild leer in her eyes.

Hark to the grating voice
   Shouting in drunken glee ;
Would she could see with sober eyes
   Her own deep misery !

A woman, did you say ?
   Woman was made to bless,
To while our cares away,
   To comfort and caress.
Oh ! who could love that face
   Begrimed by dirt and drink,
Oh ! who from that embrace
   Would not in terror shrink ?

Look at her foaming lips ;
   Hark to the muttered curse ;
A drunkard is a fiend,
   But a woman—oh ! 'tis worse !
God save the maidens fair,
   Who gaze upon her now,
From falling in the snare
   Of the fiend who has laid her low.

Only a woman drunk !
   Oh ! sons with mothers dear,
Pass her not by with a tearless eye,
   But for her drop a tear ;
Husbands with loving wives,
   Oh ! guard them well I pray,
And save them from the foul drink fiend,
   Who does all virtue slay.

Only a woman drunk !
   Once on her mother's breast,
That woman closed her baby eyes
   And sank to peaceful rest ;

And when in maiden prime,
  A bashful lover came,
And whispered words of tenderness
  Until her cheek grew flame.

Only a woman drunk!
  That woman was a wife,
And vowed to love and honor one
  And help him on through life;
And children round her knee
  Once lisped their evening prayer—
O God! that ever she
  Should lie and wallow there!

There on the pavement stone,
  Scoffed at by passers by,
Singing in drunken tone,
  With that wild leer in her eye:
Only a woman drunk!
  Brother, go home and think—
Think of your mother, sister, wife,
  And save them from the drink.

Drinking Destroys the Intellect.

OCCUPYING a place among the animated objects of nature, man is properly regarded as a member of the great family of God. But he is the constituted lord of the creation. He holds a delegated authority over the fishes of the sea, the fowls of the air, and the beasts of the earth. His authority is unlimited; and though conferred on him by the Creator of all, is yet possessed by him in consequence of that higher

nature which he sustains, and by which he is adapted
for a more exalted sphere.

Viewing the great scheme of nature in its most
comprehensive extent—embracing the reptile that
crawls in the dust and the angel that waits on the
throne of the eternal, we are gratified by the elevation that is assigned to man, while we are awed by
the responsibility which that elevation incurs.
Stationed among the beasts that perish, man partakes
of the dignity of angels. Propelled by instincts and
appetites, he knows the workings of a higher principle and feels the actings of a nobler agency. Bound
by the laws of heaven to the interests of time and
sense—engaged by the grovelling relationships of
earth, and directed to the pursuits of animal pleasures and enjoyment, he is capable of transporting
himself in thought to the highest heavens, and of con-
versing with the beings of a holier order. He forms
a resting place between the two extremes of being.
The weakness of the brute and the energy of the
angel are in him united. And is not the dignity of
man enhanced and more exalted still by the eternal
destiny with which his name is associated? Oh ! if
the pride of the human heart may be gratified and
indulged by contemplating and exerting an authority
over beings, with what feelings may the heart be ex-
panded when contemplating that dignity and glory
which belong to man as a being destined to survive
the crash of worlds and the wreck of nature ! He is
gifted with a spark of immortality, the brightness
and glory of which shall never be obscured. He is
possessed of a living principle, the vitality of which
a thousand deaths shall not injure—the vigor, the
activity, the energy of which eternity itself shall
never see impaired.

It may with propriety then be asked, whether it is not folly, the most reckless folly, for man to throw away the glory of his species and deliberately sink into the stupidity of the brute? Can there be madness more awful than that of the man who bargains his intellect, sells his reason, disposes of his whole intellectual endowments, for the short gratification of mere animal excitement? The question is neither absurd nor ridiculous. Drunkenness necessarily tends to the partial if not the perfect deprivation of intellect. It presents the eye with a spectacle more humiliating than the maniac. It exhibits an instance of suicide more painful and distressing than that of the madman. And if to human pride and independence of spirit it be humbling to behold the respectable citizen tranformed by insanity into a contemptible driveller, how painful to sober and religious contemplativeness must be the sight of the man who drowns his intellect in the cup, and banishes his reason by dissipation and debauchery! Oh! if the imbecility of the idiot humbles and depresses the mind, throws the soul back on its native dignity and powers, what painful feelings must the drunkard excite, who stupefies and maddens the brain by intoxicating draughts? We are accustomed to smile at the strange conceits and foolish extravagancies of the drunkard, but would it not be suitable to our character as men and Christians to regard him with feelings of sorrow and sympathy, and, for the instruction of our children, to point to him in pity and exclaim, behold a fool!

The Old Brandy Bottle.

[This piece will be most effectively recited in the character of a sot, his nose reddened, etc.]

THE old brandy bottle? I've loved it too long,
　It has been a false friend unto me;
When I met it at first I was healthy and strong,
　And as handsome as handsome could be.
I had plenty of cash in my pocket and purse,
　And my cheeks were as red as a rose,
And the day when I took it for better for worse,
　I'd a beautiful aquiline nose.

But now only look! I'm a sight to behold;
　The beauty I boasted has fled;
You would think I was nearly a hundred years old
　When I'm raising my hand to my head;
For it trembles and shakes like the earth when it
　　quakes,
　And I always am spilling my tea,
And whenever I speak I make awful mistakes,
　Till every one's laughing at me.

The ladies don't love me, and this I can trace
　To the loss of my aquiline nose;
Like an overgrown strawberry stuck on my face,
　Still larger and larger it grows.
And I haven't a cent in my pocket or purse,
　And my clothes are all tattered and torn;
Oh! that old brandy bottle has been a sad curse—
　And I wish I had never been born.

The old brandy bottle! I'll love it no more,
　It has near ruined my body and soul;
I'll dash it to pieces* and swear from this hour,
　To give up both it and the bowl.

　　　* Suiting the action to the words.

And I'll now go and sign—I could surely do
    worse ;
  On that pledge all my hopes I repose ;
And I'll get back my money in pocket and purse,
  And also my beautiful nose.

The Dying Girl.

LOOK how redly glows the sunset on the treetops in
    the lane ;
Lift my head a little, mother, I may never see it
    again—
I may die before the morning, for I have been lying
    long,
And some weeks have dragged on, mother, since you
    thought that I was gone.

On that dull, cold evening, mother, when I lay so
    still and white,
And you told poor father I was dead, when he came
    home at night ;
And he came and knelt beside my bed, and his voice
    was deep and low,
And he prayed a little prayer, mother, as he used to,
    long ago.

And he promised you he'd stay at home to comfort
    you at night,
And help you walk the thorny road that leads to
    realms of light.
For he thought that I was even there, but I have not
    gone yet ;
But I am going soon, mother—be sure you do not
    fret.

I hope he won't be late to-night : I should so like to
    see
His face once more, and hear his voice just say
    " Good-bye " to me.
I'd ask him then to promise me—and I do think he
    would—
That he would never drink again, but help you to be
    good.

And I'm sure he'd keep his word—he always did to
    me ;
And, mother, when I am in heaven, I could look
    down and see
How happy you were living, free from drink and all
    its care,
And I would stand close to the gate, and wait for
    you both there.

Hark, mother ! I can hear his feet upon the gravel
    walk ;
Father, dear father, come to me, I want a little talk.
Now stand beside my bed—just here—and lay your
    hand in mine.
The sun has gone to sleep at last—I shall not see it
    shine.

When I am gone, my father dear, and mother is
    alone—
When I am lying quietly beneath the churchyard
    stone,
I want you now to promise me you will not stay out
    late ;
And, though the men should ask you, don't go in the
    green gate.

But stay at home with mother dear, and talk to her
    of me,
That where I soon am going you, too, may also be.
And go to church on Sunday—you used to like to go,
And sit in that old-fashioned pew where we sat long
    ago.

And read your Bible, father dear, at morning and at
    night,
So that I can come very near, though hid from
    human sight.
And I shall hear your voice repeat those words of
    love and peace,
About the land I soon shall see, where sorrows all
    shall cease.

You will, my father! say you will! Oh, bless you for
    that word!
It is the sweetest sound that my poor ears have ever
    heard.
My mother, I can leave you now, for father will be
    kind;
You must not fret, my mother dear, when you are
    left behind.

So take my head upon your breast, and put your
    hand in mine—
A light is breaking in the sky—the light of love
    divine!
I see that white-robed throng again, with crowns
    upon each brow;
Make way, make way, ye angel bands, I come to join
    you now!

THE AMERICAN

TEMPERANCE SPEAKER

No. 1.

A CHOICE COLLECTION OF

DIALOGUES, PROSE AND POETRY,

ESPECIALLY ADAPTED FOR USE IN ALL

Adult and Juvenile Temperance Organizations,

SABBATH AND DAY SCHOOLS,

AND FOR

PUBLIC AND PRIVATE READINGS, RECITATIONS AND ADDRESSES.

Compiled by *J. S. OGILVIE.*

NEW YORK:

American Temperance Publishing House,

29 ROSE STREET,

1879.

TEMPERANCE DRAMAS.

Price Fifteen Cents Each.

☞ ALL Organizations would do well to preserve this list for future reference. It is the only complete list ever published.

Another Glass.—A Drama in 1 Act   By Thomas Morton. 6 Male. 3 Female characters. Costumes English, modern. A very effective Temperance play. Scenery necessary. Time of representation, one hour.

Aunt Dinah's Pledge.—Drama in 2 Acts.   By Harry Seymour. (New Edition, Revised and Improved.) 6 Male and 3 Female characters. Scenery and properties easy. Costumes of the present day. Very effective play. Time of representation, one hour.

Bottle, The.—Drama in 2 Acts and 8 Tableaux.   By T. P. Taylor. 11 Male, 6 Female characters. Costumes and properties simple, but scenery somewhat difficult. Time of representation, about two hours and a half.

Closing of the "Eagle," The.—A Drama in 4 Acts.   By H. Elliott McBride. 4 Male and 2 Female characters. Costumes, modern. Scenes, parlor and bar-room. Time of representation, one hour and fifteen minutes.

Don't Marry a Drunkard to Reform Him.—A Drama in 5 Acts.   By H. Elliott McBride. 8 Male and 3 Female characters. Costumes, modern. Scene, rooms neatly and poorly furnished and bar-room. Time of representation, one hour and thirty minutes.

Drop too Much, A.—Farce in 1 Scene. 4 Male, 2 Female characters. Two Yankees, Irishman, walking gent, old woman and Yankee girl. Temperance farce. Time of representation, thirty minutes.

Drunkard, The; or, The Fallen Saved.—Drama in 5 Acts. Adapted by Wm. H. Smith. 13 Male, 5 Female characters. Properties easy. Costumes of the present day. A great deal of scenery required, but none of it of a very elaborate nature. Time of representation, about two hours and a half.

Drunkard's Children, The.—Drama in 2 Acts.   By J. B. Johnstone. 20 Male, 6 Female characters. Costumes and properties not very difficult, but scenery rather elaborate. Time of representation, about one hour and a half.

Drunkard's Doom, The; or, The Last Nail.—Romantic Drama in 2 Acts. By G. D. Pitt. 15 Male, 5 Female characters. Costumes, properties, and scenery very elaborate. Time of representation, one hour and a half.

Drunkard's Home, The.—A Drama in 2 Acts. 13 Male, 6 Female characters. Costumes modern. Properties easy. Scenes, interiors and exteriors. Time of representation, about two hours.

Drunkard's Warning, The.—Drama in 3 Acts.   By C. W. Taylor. 6 Male, 3 Female characters. Scenery and properties simple. Costumes, modern. This play is a general favorite among amateurs. Time of representation, about one hour and three-quarters.

Fatal Glass, The; or, The Curse of Drink.—Drama in 3 Acts. By James McCloskey. 11 Male, 8 Female characters. Costumes, easy; but properties and scenery, especially the latter, very difficult. A very effective play for the regular stage. Time of representation, about two hours.

Fifteen Years of a Drunkard's Life.—Melodrama in 3 Acts. By Douglas Jerrold. (New Edition, revised and improved.) 10 Male, 4 Female characters. Costumes modern. Properties, simple. Scenery somewhat elaborate. Time of representation, about one hour and three-quarters.

Fruits of the Wine-Cup.—Drama in 3 Acts..   By Jno. H. Allen. 6 Male, 8 Female characters. Costumes modern. Properties simple. Scenery easily arranged. An excellent play for amateur performance. Time of representation, about one hour and twenty minutes.

Game of Billiards, A.—Sketch in 1 Act.   By McDermott and Trumble. 1 Male, 2 Female characters. Costumes modern. Scene easy. Time of representation, twenty minutes.

Last Drop, The.—Drama in 1 Act.   By John H. Delafield. 7 Male, 8 Female characters. Costumes modern. Scenes, a plain room, a street, and a garret. Time of representation, twenty-five minutes.

Last Loaf, The.—Drama in 2 Acts. 5 Male, 3 Female characters. Leading man, juvenile, two low comedians, villain, leading lady, walking lady, and soubrette. This drama is intensely interesting as a Temperance drama. Time of representation, one hour and thirty minutes.

Address **J. S. OGILVIE, Publisher, 29 Rose St., New York.**

American Temperance Publishing House.

TEMPERANCE LECTURES

BY

JOHN B. GOUGH.

Price, 10 cents each.

The American Temperance Publishing House have just commenced publishing a series of lectures on Temperance, and now announce that the first three given by that prince of orators, John B. Gough, are ready. Mr. Gough needs no introduction or recommendation. His name is a household word in this and other lands, and we are glad to be able to offer to the many thousands who have been unable to listen to his burning words of eloquence these lectures, in the hope that his influence may reach and aid many who are struggling against the monster of strong drink.

Each lecture contains 24 pages, in paper cover, and is illustrated by a fine wood engraving of Mr. Gough, and also his autograph, which alone is worth the price of the pamphlet.

No. 1. OUR BATTLE CRY: TOTAL ABSTINENCE.
No. 2. THE FORCE OF APPETITE.
No. 3. THE ONLY REMEDY.

Price 10 cts. each; per doz., $1.00. The three lectures in one pamphlet, price 25 cts.

Special rates will be given for cheap editions on thin paper for general distribution. No better work can be done by any organization or individual than to place a copy of each of these lectures in every family in their community. Other lectures by Mr. Gough and other eminent men will soon follow.

AUTOBIOGRAPHY AND PERSONAL RECOLLECTIONS

OF

JOHN B. GOUGH.

Comprising a complete history of his eventful life, an account of his childhood in England, with thrilling details of his almost superhuman struggles against intemperance! His wretched condition and final victory; his labors in behalf of Temperance; his first speech, together with an account of his experience and success as a lecturer. Also, vivid pen paintings of what he saw and heard in England. The whole enlivened by anecdotes, affecting incidents, and personal experiences, many of which are amusing, interesting, and full of pathos, and which no one can describe better than Mr. Gough.

The aim of the author in writing this book has been to give a full history of his life, from his birth and childhood in England to his arrival in this country; his course of dissipation, with an account of his reformation, subsequent breaking of the pledge, and the terrible experience of September, 1845. Also, his career as a public speaker, cases of reform through his labors, his first and last visit to England. A full history of his work, reaching on to the present time, and concluding with an account of the celebration of the "Silver Wedding" of Mr. and Mrs. Gough, at their home near Worcester.

The work is published in a handsome octavo volume of 550 pages, on fine white paper, printed from electrotype plates, and is embellished by an elegant portrait of Mr. Gough, engraved on steel, and other illustrations by George Cruikshank and other eminent artists, and is bound in neat and substantial binding. Prices: Extra English cloth binding, beautiful white paper, **$3.25** ; leather binding, **$3.75**; half calf binding, **$4.50.**

This book cannot be had except through the publisher's agents. Sent by mail, postpaid, to any address on receipt of price. Agents wanted to canvass for it, to whom the most liberal terms are offered. Send for particulars.

Address **J. S. OGILVIE, Publisher, 29 Rose St., New York.**